FINAL

SHELBYDOG CHRONICLES

FINAL
SHELBYDOG CHRONICLES

Touched by a Dog

Mark G. Boyer

RESOURCE *Publications* · Eugene, Oregon

FINAL SHELBYDOG CHRONICLES
Touched by a Dog

Resource Publications
An Imprint of Wipf and Stock Publishers
199 W. 8th Ave., Suite 3
Eugene, OR 97401

www.wipfandstock.com

PAPERBACK ISBN: 979-8-3852-6105-5
HARDCOVER ISBN: 979-8-3852-6106-2
EBOOK ISBN: 979-8-3852-6107-9

VERSION NUMBER 101325

Dedicated to
Michelle Phillips,
dog whisperer,

and to Shelbydog Cole,
2012–2025,
faithful companion

Everything comes from God in order to return to God.[*]

God creates himself in an ineffable manner in his creation; he manifests himself and from being invisible he becomes visible.[*]

Each existent thing goes on existing only so far as it expresses the Idea from which it emanates; and it expresses this Idea so far as it contemplates it.[*]

... [T]he value of the creature is only the reflection and the effect of the value of the Creator.[*]

Created things are only the reflection of the divine thought.[*]

* Philippe Delhaye, *Medieval Christian Philosophy* (New York: Hawthorn Books, 1960), pages 35, 56, 58, 83, and 103.

CONTENTS

INTRODUCTION

IN 2020, CORBIN S. Cole and I wrote *Living Parables: Today's Versions* (Eugene, OR: Wipf & Stock), and we dedicated the book to "Shelbydog, a living parable, brindle-sparkling-in-the-sun red, four-footed funny companion on the journey, and a mystical burning bush in our midst—an image of the Divine." Cole, a former student and good friend, had rescued Shelby from the local Human Society and would bring her with him when he came to my home to work on the book and to eat dinner. After getting married to Dani, they decided to move to Florida, but Shelby, who I had named Shelbydog, was not able to go with them, because she could not tolerate the humidity. From the day Cole adopted her, it was clear that she was an inside dog. Thus, before they left for Florida, they announced to me that they were giving Shelbydog to me. While she had been living with me off and on—I was frequently dog sitting her for the Coles—she became my dog in 2020. I never changed her last name; I merely added *dog* to her first name to form a new first name: Shelbydog.

I began keeping *The Shelbydog Chronicles* on August 26, 2019. Written on 50-sheet 8" x 11" note pads, the nine volumes from August 26, 2019, to June 30, 2025, contain my day-to-day experiences with Shelbydog, and became the sources for the two books that I wrote about her: *The Shelbydog Chronicles by Shelby Cole As Recorded by Mark G. Boyer: A Novel* (Eugene, OR: Resource Publications, Wipf & Stock, 2022) and *More Shelbydog Chronicles: Reflections on a Dog's Life by Her Friend, Knowing Your Pet* (Eugene, OR: Resource Publications, Wipf & Stock, 2024). *The Shelbydog Chronicles* were written from Shelbydog's point of view. *More Shelbydog Chronicles* was written from my point of view, although she wrote the Introduction to the book. As already indicated in the Dedication above, Shelbydog died on June 30, 2025, and I felt compelled to write this final volume in the trilogy: *Final Shelbydog Chronicles*. In the pages that follow I show how a Labrado-Boxer mix, weighing sixty pounds, not only affected me and many of the people living in my neighborhood, but many others as a silent missionary. Most of the people who met Shelby were *Touched by a Dog.*

1

UPDATES ON SHELBYDOG 2023–2024

2023

AUGUST 2023 FOUND SHELBYDOG and me in an apartment over a three-car garage seven-miles outside Fairplay, Colorado. We had spent the month of August 2022 there, and both of us enjoyed it enough to make plans with the owner to occupy the apartment in 2023. It was located at 9,300 feet, which meant that the daytime temperatures never rose over seventy degrees Fahrenheit and the nights were very cool (often dropping to close to freezing). I spent the days writing and reading, and Shelbydog spent the days sitting in a large over-stuffed chair gazing through a double window watching the crows fly by, the aspen leaves dance in the wind, the white, puffy clouds float along, and looking for any other kind of wildlife that might appear on the mountain side. She often spent a few hours on the stoop in the sun.

In August 2023, Shelbydog and I were navigating the steps from the ground to the apartment, walking the quarter-mile lane to the main road and back a few times a day, and walking around the property, all the while she was wearing a brace to support her front paws and shoulders. While she had a slight limp before, it had gotten worse; with the double-brace support she was able to return to her active life. I put it on her—she was a dog who liked to wear things!—before going out for walks, and I took it off of her once we got back.

As early as April 2023 I realized that Shelbydog was having acid reflux at night. I had listened as she smacked her lips at times during the night. I had seen the spots on her bed where she had tried to lick it off her tongue. So, after giving her antacid tablets for a short time and doing some online research about dogs and acid reflux, I began to give her an Omeprazole capsule before her breakfast. Of course, as with any other medicine she took, I had to wrap it in soft, canned dogfood so she could not see or smell it and serve it to her in a small bowl so she could not spit it out without me seeing it or place it in her bowl with her kibble. Before the Omeprazole, I had tried Nexium, which gave her diarrhea, and antacid tablets, which did not work throughout the day and night.

By late April 2023, I had the acid reflux under control. What I didn't have under control was Shelbydog's often diarrhea. We had been through the white rice with boiled chicken plan after fasting for a day several times. We had seen her veterinarian, who gave her two different medications to arrest the diarrhea. Even with the diarrhea, Shelbydog wanted to walk a mile three times a day, when we went outside.

Through experimentation, I discovered that both of us slept better at night, when I ran the fan, and on warmer nights, the window air conditioner in our bedroom. Shelbydog's bed was next to my twin bed. Because she liked to sleep with a blanket, she stayed warm until she wiggled out from under it. Often, she would awaken me during the night with a paw on my bed. I'd lean over and see that she was uncovered, find her blanket, and recover her. The noise of the fan or air conditioner drowned out other night noises in the city where we lived. That enabled both of us to get a good night's sleep.

In May 2023, Shelbydog and I were walking a good mile in the morning, another mile after lunch, and a shorter walk after diner. With the help of her veterinarian, I had determined that it was better for her to eat three meals a day than it was to feed her all her food at one time. Her veterinarian had advised me to count her calories, rather than the amount of food she was getting, and divide them by three in order to determine what she needed to have three times a day. At this time, she was still very active; so, she ate a half-cup of kibble, a large dog bone, a piece of chicken jerky, and a small dog bone at each of three meals. As she decreased in activity, she got a third-cup of kibble with the usual bones. After she ate her dinner, she got a brushing chew, which was one of her favorite bones. She would take it from my hand with her mouth and go to lie on one of her favorite rugs in the house, where she would place it between her front paws so that it leaned slightly to her left and she could bite off pieces until it was all gone.

During 2023, Shelbydog was happy. She indicated it by stopping in the grass during walks, throwing herself onto the grass, and rolling from side to side, twisting her head and body while lying on her back, and rolling from side to side again and again. If she stopped on an incline, she would roll to the sidewalk. Inside the house, she chose a large rug in the living room to do the same. Along with a smiling face, she also indicated her happiness with heavy breathing.

When we visited friends who lived in a two-story house, Shelbydog liked to run up the front steps, across the second story, and come down the back steps. All in the house could hear her as her paws' nails click-clicked across the wood floors. At home, I usually knew where she was because of the click-click of her nails on my tile floors.

As 2023 continued to warm and the humidity came in from the Gulf of Mexico, Shelbydog began to slow, especially outside. Often, we cut our walks short, because she would stop for a few seconds, raise her nose in the air while thinking, and then turn around and head for home. Also, her legs were getting stiff. While she had always spent time stretching before going for a walk, she spent more time getting ready by extending her front paws in front of her and bowing her head to the floor. I didn't know it then, but hip dysplasia was also taking place.

Near the end of May 2023 we were visiting friends. I had put Shelby into her bed and covered her with her blanket, while I went to the bathroom to bush my teeth and get ready to get into my bed. When I came back from the bathroom to our bedroom, Shelby was in my bed with her head on my pillow. And she was smiling. After I laughed, I embraced her, kissed her, and lifted her out of my bed and placed her in her own bed. When we traveled, I had attempted to let her sleep beside me when we had a large bed in our motel room; however, she usually squirmed around during the night and pushed against me with all four feet to move me out of her way. I came close to falling out of bed several times and, after those experiences, brought Shelbydog's travel bed in which she slept. The first time I brought it in, she didn't like it that she could not sleep next to me, but after a couple times it became a part of her routine.

By June 2023, her arthritis was affecting her a lot. When I took off her harness in the evening after our last trip outside, one night as I lifted her paw to slip the harness strap over it, she squealed a little; that is how I knew she was in pain. Her veterinarian had given her Carprofen to be used occasionally, but after that experience I began to administer it to her two times a day. While she spent the mornings in the sun on the front porch behind the glass door, she would get out of the sun when hot, and lie on the tile floor on the porch or come into the house and lie on the tile floor in front of an air conditioning vent; she knew where all of them were throughout the house! Because of the high humidity, Shelbydog didn't want to walk too far.

We spent the month of August 2023 outside Fairplay, Colorado, in the apartment over a three-car garage. At 9,300 feet, the days were cool and the nights were often cold. Shelbydog loved it. I worked on books, while she stretched out in the sun on the stoop at the top of the stairs outside our front door. With her brace on, Shelbydog was able to walk slowly down the lane from the main road and to get into and out of her overstuffed chair easily; she had stopped jumping and was lowering her front paws to the floor and then lowering her back paws from the chair to the floor. It kept her from aggravating her arthritis. During that month, we entertained visitors, enjoyed sleep-ins, and lying beside me on the bed a few times as long as I lifted her onto the bed and took her off. With some friends and wearing her brace she came along for a hike; she was fine as long as we stopped frequently and gave her plenty of water to drink.

After getting down the stairs and going for a walk, she was still able to move up the steps slowly. She would run two-thirds of the way up the stairs, where she would have to stop to catch her breath after taking each step one at a time. She was aging before my eyes.

When not in the sun on the stoop, Shelby spent most of her day in the overstuffed chair in front of the double windows. She was very creative in figuring out how to fit herself in the chair. She could curl into a ball and fit in the seat. She could lay her head on either arm and fit into the seat. She could place her front legs on the back of the chair and lay her head either on her paws or on the chair's back between her front paws and watch through the window. When she was curled into a ball, she could lean her head off the edge of the seat of the chair without falling off!

That chair must have been easier on her aches and pains than her bed, because she slept many nights in that chair, or slept a while in it and then came to her bed. The last days before we left, there was a full moon, and

Shelbydog spent most of the nights in her chair gazing at it through the windows. That month Shelbydog was able to walk, hike, rest, and sleep.

Because of her occasional diarrhea, in September 2023, I did some online research and found Bernie's Perfect Poop, a petfood additive that stopped diarrhea by hardening her stool. I bought a package of it, began putting a teaspoon full of the granulated additive on Shelbydog's food, and discovered that it stopped the diarrhea completely. After being home about a week, we had another trip to take. Later in the month, Shelbydog became very uncooperative due to the humidity, heat, and rain. In other words, she was irritable. After a block on a walk, she would turn around and want to go home. If it had rained and the sidewalk was damp, she would turn around after only a few blocks. At times, she was also moving very slowly and limping severely when walking. Our daily three walks diminished to only a few blocks at a time. Of course, on cooler days, she might go farther. While moderating how far I thought she could go, I often let her go farther, and I often stopped and turned her around, when I thought she was going farther than she could walk home. By mid-October 2023, if she walked too far, ran, or trotted one day, her limp was worse the next day.

By the end of October 2023, Shelbydog was wearing her double brace all day, and we were walking only one square block in the morning and a half block after lunch and dinner. Often, she wanted to go farther, but it was too hard on her; so, I had to turn her around and head home. Even with the brace on, she often stumbled. When it was raining, I would put her coat on her and take her to the back yard, where she could pee and poop; I knew that she would not walk if she felt a drop of rain on her head!

In early November 2023, after making the time change, we began a short outing around 4 p.m. with a quick front yard session for her to pee at 6:30 p.m. After that I would remove her bandana, brace, and harness, and she would lie on her pallet on the front porch. I'd cover her with a blanket, and she would sleep until I called her to come to bed. I'd go to our bedroom, turn on lights, and get myself ready for bed, while waiting on Shelbydog to come in. Usually, she came in a few minutes, but sometimes I had to go get her on the front porch. After she got comfortable lying on her pallet, she fell asleep and didn't want to have to get up and walk to the bedroom!

By the end of November 2023, Shelbydog was still able to walk down the steps with her brace on and, after a short walk, pee and poop. When I was working at a desk on the sunporch, she was able to walk down the back steps slowly, spend time with me, and then walk up the steps to her favorite room: the front porch. Cloudy days found her restless and roaming around the house. She was beginning to have more pain and needed painkillers twice a day to keep her comfortable. Because her bed was more comfortable than her front porch pallet, she often went to bed immediately after we came in from her last pee-pee session for the day and after I removed her bandana, brace, and harness. Often, she would stop and look back to see if I was following her to cover her with her blanket once she got into her bed.

After years and years of not liking to get a bath, by December 2023, Shelby would get excited when I began mentioning it a few days before it was scheduled to occur. After I gathered her towels and shampoo and placed extra rugs on the bathroom floor, I'd call her, and she would come and stand in front of the shower. Sometimes, she would come to the bathroom without even being called. After removing her bandana and brace, I would use her harness to lift her into the shower, remove the harness, gently wet her with the removeable shower nozzle, then spread her shampoo for dogs with sensitive skin all over her, rub it in, and then rinse it off. She tended to want to shake herself, but I repeated, "No shaking!" After she dripped for a minute or so, I would place a towel over her and begin to dry her. She would step out of the shower, and I would take a dry towel and dry the remaining wet parts. I'd open the bathroom door, and she would walk to the front porch, where I followed with a towel to dry her belly and legs after rolling her on her side. I also taught her not to fear the hair dryer. I would call her back to the bathroom, saying, "Shelbydog, let me dry you a little more," and she would sit on the bathroom rug while I dried her fur with the hair dryer set on cool; it if was set on warm, she would get up and leave.

Along with other experiences, Shelbydog and I trusted each other. She trusted me with the hair dryer and with her medicine. She trusted me to prepare her food, to put on her harness, brace, bandana, and coat, when needed. Especially after a snowfall, she trusted me to lead her on our usual paths, which were difficult to see with snow on them.

By February 2024, Shelbydog had rallied and was feeling well, but she often overdid it. She watched tree trimmers cut down a very large, old pine tree in the neighbor's yard, after snow and ice had broken off branches. She wanted to be outside with me when I was talking to the neighbors. The tree trimmers had an unleashed dog around, and that dog and Shelby played and ran around the yard. Shelbydog overdid it, and she was in pain that evening. I had to give her Tramadol; her veterinarian had given it to her for severe pain. Throughout the month of February 2024, her limp worsened, and I gave her Tramadol to ease the pain. She couldn't walk very far, and there were several times when she stopped and couldn't move. I'd lift her into my arms and carry her home. I spent a lot of time praying for her healing. She didn't like being carried down the steps, on the sidewalk, or up the steps, but there was nothing else I could do. I began intensifying her Movoflex regiment. In addition to the Advanced Movoflex at dinner, I began to give her the regular Movoflex with breakfast and lunch. She still needed Tramadol from time to time, but she rallied again.

A few days before Christmas 2023, she went with me to a neighbor's wine and cheese party and spent most of her time lying at my feet under the table at which I was sitting. On Christmas morning we joined other friends for breakfast.

In one *Chronicles* entry I noted that Shelbydog possessed a quiet dignity that needed to be respected. I wanted to respect it, honor it, love it, and recognize it, because it connected me to a greater universal dignity. The more I reflected on that, I came to understand that Shelbydog's dignity came from God. She was a creature to be respected, as she disclosed the divine to everyone she met.

2024

In early January 2024, Shelbydog was feeling good. She possessed the amazing ability to rally. She was playing, wanting to run on walks, finding me in the house, begging for bellyrubs, making noises to get my attention. In the afternoons, she would leave her front porch and come lie on the living room rug, while I sat reading in a chair. After lying on the rug, she would roll from side to side and wiggle her whole body in delight. She even created a game. After wiggling for a while, she would come and lie on the floor by my chair and put one of her front feet on another chair close by. I'd reach over and take her paw off the other chair. Then, she would put it there again, and I'd remove it again. I'd scratch her ears or touch her neck. She would relax. Then, she would begin with the foot again. We would play that game for ten to fifteen minutes. Then, she would get tired, get up, and go back to the front porch.

Another game she liked to play concerned coming to bed. Our usual routine consisted of me awakening her on her pallet on the front porch and turning on the light. I'd tell her that it was time for bed, then I would go to our bedroom and turn on the lights and pull down the covers on my bed. While brushing my teeth, Shelby would come click-click-clicking on the tile floor. I'd stop what I was doing, go to her in her bed, pray with her, kiss her on the head, and tell her how much I loved her, cover her with her blanket, and then finish what I was doing, go lock the front door, and go to bed. However, there were times when she walked softly and I didn't hear her going to bed. After brushing me teeth, I headed to the front porch, but she was not there! After turning off the light and locking the door, I walked to the bedroom, and there she was already in bed, usually curled into a brindle fur ball and often already asleep. She was a rascal at times!

Once such rascal time in January 2024 was her presence in the living room, where I was sitting and reading, and solicitation for a bellyrub. Just as I was beginning the bellyrub, she got up and headed to the back door. "Do you need to go outside?" I asked her, and she headed further to the back door. We went outside; she had some diarrhea, something that still happened only occasionally. When we got back into the house, I gave her some of her anti-diarrhea medicine.

Another occasional rascal incident occurred a few days later. After going out the front door for her final pee of the day, we came in and I took off her bandana, brace, and harness. She went to her front porch, looked through the front door, turned around, and went to bed. I followed her, prayed with her, kissed her, and covered her with her blanket, while saying, "You rascal, Shelbydog."

Another day in early January, after I gave Shelbydog a bath, she joined me at a desk on the back sunporch. I was proofreading some manuscript pages, and she laid on a rug by my chair. I reached over and petted her, discovered that her butt was still damp. I said, "Let's go back to the bathroom, and I'll hair-dry your butt." I went to the bathroom, and she followed. I hair-dried her butt. She sat very still, while I moved the cool-blowing air around her body. When I finished, she went back to her front porch.

It snowed and turned so bitterly cold in January 2024 that all we could do was go to the backyard a few times a day for Shelbydog's necessary peeing and pooping. She didn't want to stay outside very long. Quickly, she did her business, turned around, and headed for the back door. Likewise, she didn't fall asleep on the front porch in the evenings; she would come to the living room, and I would cover her with a blanket, and it wasn't long before I heard snoring.

Often, I would tell Shelbydog, "Go sit on your rug, and I'll get you ready for your walk." What I meant was for her to go to the rug in the doorway between the dining room and the living room. I had placed a new rug by my chair in the dining room for her to sit and lie on. After giving her the usual command, I looked at her seated on the rug by my chair. I had to laugh, because she did what I had told her to do—she went and sat on a rug. It just wasn't the rug I intended for her to sit on!

In the summertime, when coming back into the house after getting hot, Shelbydog would find a place on the floor in front of a vent emitting cool (conditioned) air. She knew where all the vents in the living room, dining room, and office were located, and she would place herself before one of them until she cooled. Then, she would go to her front porch.

Because she was feeling good, she was very cooperative. Because there was sunshine and some warmth, we were able to take a couple of walks. I put her coat on her and used the sling to get her down the front steps. Snow had melted off most of the sidewalks, and she enjoyed being in the crisp, fresh air. I was amazed how cooperative she was. The bond we shared was getting deeper, and both of us recognized it. In other words, our respect for each other was obvious.

With the medicine her veterinarian gave her, Shelbydog was feeling even better. There were many nights in late January 2024, when she voluntarily went to bed early and mornings when the slept until 10 or 11 a.m.

In early February 2024, I noted how the trust between me and Shelbydog had grown. Trust is important to me, and it was important to Shelbydog. She trusted me to give her her medicines, to feed her, to walk her, to cover her, to bathe her, etc. I trusted her to cooperate by taking the medicine she watched me hide in canned dog food, to eat her meals, to walk with me, to help me give her a bath, to come to bed when I called her, and more. The only problem we had was her stubborn determination to walk further than I knew she could. I would stop, when I thought we had gone far enough, tell her it was time to turn around, and stand facing the direction we needed to go to get home. While she would pull the leash the opposite direction, I keep saying, "Shelbydog, this way." After repeating that, she would relinquish, turn around, and head home with me.

Also in February 2024, Shelbydog had lots of visitors. The Kimmons Family from a few blocks down the street, made frequent visits to her. She was an expert at soliciting bellyrubs from them. Also, she got a daily visit from our mail carrier, Jared, and, after he left, from his wife, Misti, who gave her more bellyrubs. She would greet them as they entered the front porch. Then, she would put herself close to them to solicit pettings and bellyrubs. After a while, they would have to leave to continue their mail delivery route. People made Shelbydog tired. After they left, she would stretch herself on a rug and fall asleep.

She loved to travel with me, even on short errands around town. In the wintertime, she always went along, because the car would stay cool. It was difficult in the summer, because the car would get hot and stay hot, and I had to leave her at home most of the time. She always went with me to the airport to pick up one of her favorite people and visitors: Matthew. As soon as he would get in the front passenger seat, she would lean over and smell him, then she would smile. He spent a lot of time petting her, talking to her, bellyrubbing her, and walking her. When he was around, she wanted to spend all her time with him. It was important that she go with us, when it was time to take him back to the airport. That way she knew he was gone, but that didn't stop her from being sad after he left.

By late February 2024, Shelbydog's limp had gotten worse. Not only was it affecting her outside, it was affecting her inside the house. I gave her Tramadol for her pain, and we cut back on how far we walked. There were times, even on short walks, when Shelbydog had to stop, sit, and rest a while. There were also times, when I had to gather her into my arms and carry her home. I prayed for her healing and/or a peaceful death during her sleep. However, after a few days, Shelby rallied. Her limp disappeared. Her rascality was evident when she slipped by me at the front door, bounded down the steps, and stopped so I could put on her leash. She didn't like being picked up and carried, and I knew that. I concluded that God was healing his servant, Shelbydog, rather than accepting her spirit, although at the end of February I was getting up during the night—after listening to Shelbydog sleep restlessly moving around in her bed—to give her a Tramadol, because I concluded that she was in pain. Usually, she would then sleep for a few more hours.

In March 2024, Shelby was feeling well and walking a square block at least once a day. She was taking Carprofen and Tramadol, and she was energized and active. Only very warm March days seemed to slow her. She was busy lying in the sunshine, going outside to see what was happening, following me and visitors through the house, and going up and down steps in the front and the back of the house. All the activity activated her limp again. So, we began to walk slowly and to take shorter walks. Meanwhile, I was praying that she be healed by God—a mighty deed, a miracle—or that the divine receive her spirit. She was approaching her twelfth birthday, and she had had a good life. Her veterinarian answered an e-mail I sent her, asking about what else I could do for Shelbydog, by telling me to stick to the plan; she offered other pain medication if needed. Many of Shelbydog's friends stopped by to visit her. Her usual routine after her friends left was to go to the living room and play with her pillow; it was a way that she dissipated some of her excitement and energy, so she could take a nap. Otherwise, she spent a lot of time with me wherever I was in the house.

After changing from standard time to daylight savings time, Shelby-dog was confused. Her circadian rhythms told her it was time to eat, but that was standard time; or her circadian rhythms told her it was time for bed, but there was still daylight outside. By mid-March she had rallied again. She was not limping, but she did stumble occasionally while walk-ing. We were walking a square block three times a day, and Shelbydog was very happy, even being wild and crazy at times. She was taking Carprofen twice a day, restorative chews three times a day, and allergy medicine once a day along with Omeprazole once a day. I was thanking God every day for healing his servant, Shelbydog.

In late March, Shelbydog was getting lots of visitors from the neigh-borhood. Even Corbin, who had rescued her from the shelter, stopped in to see her with his wife and son. She was happy to see them, and kept going back and forth from one to another to solicit ear scratchings and bellyrubs. She was without pain, but very tired when they left. She got up early the next morning, but went back to bed shortly thereafter for a few more hours of sleep. Then, she spent the day lying on her pallet on the front porch. I concluded that her little bit of diarrhea that day was due to the anxiety she had the day before with many people visiting her.

On April 7, 2024, Shelbydog turned 12 (equivalent to 77 human years). She enjoyed the sunshine and being outside with me, but she was very tired after roaming around the yard. By mid-April she was getting up early, walking to her front door to see what was going on outside, then coming to me to be petted and wait until there was enough daylight to see to walk. Sometimes, after I scratched her ears for a while, she went back to bed and slept for a few more hours. We were taking three walks a day. The increased humidity was causing her not to walk very far. Because I thought she might be in pain, I was giving her Tramadol on a more regular basis.

One morning in mid-April, she awakened me at 4 a.m. sitting in front of our bedroom door. I got up, opened the door, and followed her to the front door. I knew she wanted me to open the front door so she could go sit on the front porch, so I did. She wanted me to follow her. When we got on the front porch, I saw that it was raining, lightening, and heard the thunder. I had taught Shelbydog not to be afraid of thunder by sitting behind her in front of the glass door and watching it rain, lightning, and listening to it thunder, while telling her, "Nothing will hurt you." So, at her urging, we did that again, and it made her very comfortable and happy. After about twenty minutes, the thunderstorm passed, and both of us went back to bed.

Shelbydog had her annual veterinarian visit in late April 2024. She demonstrated her rascality by not pooping that morning, even though the veterinarian wanted a poop sample. She cooperated with the blood draw and other shots and liquids that her veterinarian gave her. Because we were not walking as far as we had been, Shelbydog's toe nails were long. The veterinarian sent in a staff member to cut them. I was ready for anything, but Shelbydog just laid on her side and let the staff member clip her nails. She didn't move, and I was amazed! I was expecting that she would pull away her paws, because she did not like having her paws held.

By May 2024, our walking consisted of one square block a day and two shorter walks—sometimes just a few feet—so she could pee and poop. If it were humid or warm or raining, Shelbydog would do her business quickly, turn around, and head home. There were many days of rain in May 2024, and Shelbydog was sad when it rained. Her friends would cheer her, when they came to visit her. They liked to sit in a circle around her on a large rug, and she would move from one to another to be petted and bellyrubbed. She also enjoyed the attention she got from men working on my home. While she would enter the new room being built, she did not stay very long, because she did not feel safe in it.

In late May 2024, I bought Shelbydog a ramp to use to get into the back of the Jeep and out again. It only took a few attempts before she knew how to use it. She was more confident walking up into the Jeep or walking down the ramp from the Jeep to the garage floor if I stood straddling the ramp with my hands on either side of her as she made her way up or down. See, Shelbydog just couldn't walk in a straight line! I was giving her Tramadol frequently, because her limp was appearing more often. The high humidity drained her of energy, and she often turned around on walks and headed back home. While I tried to get her outside to walk early in the morning before the humidity got high, because of her limp, she did not want to go very far. She was cutting short her walks, and I was giving her Tramadol for the pain which I thought she had. Near the end of the month, there were several times where she stopped, and I had to elevate her into my arms and carry her a short distance or all the way home.

In early June 2024, Shelbydog rallied. By taking Carprofen and Tramadol her pain was under control, and she was playing, walking, running, rolling, and resting comfortably. She loved the cool, low-humidity mornings we were having in June. She liked a workman named Luke, because he talked to her and petted her. She tried to get Braedon to pay attention to her by bringing him her toys, but he just walked by her. Another worker appeared—Chris—and he talked to her and petted her. And that made her happy. In mid-June she had many visitors, and they wore her out. She brought them her toys and solicited bellyrubs from all of them. One afternoon, she fell asleep after everyone left.

When the humidity returned, so did Shelbydog's limp. I gave her Tramadol to mitigate the pain. I knew it was working, because she was happily stopping to roll in the grass, when we went for short walks. One evening in mid-June, while working on bookshelves in the basement, I came upstairs to go to bed and found Shelbydog already in bed. So, I turned on the window air conditioner, prayed with her, kissed her on the head, covered her with her blanket, brushed my teeth, and went to bed. On another night she came to the basement and spent some time with me, while I was watching a DVD. She solicited bellyrubs for a while, but when I stopped, she went back to her front porch. That June was very hot and humid with feel-like temperatures over one hundred degrees.

July 2024 found me preparing for our trip in August. Shelbydog was still able to get down the back steps to see what the handyman was doing outside. Some of her friends she had not seen in a long time came by to visit her, and she got one's attention by jumping on him in excitement. After entertaining guests in mid-July the evening before, both Shelbydog and I slept in the next morning. Both of us are introverts, and people wear us out. She was able to walk a square block most mornings, while it was cool and before the humidity came back. After the walk and she ate her breakfast, it was not unusual for her to go back to bed and sleep for an hour or so. In mid-July her sling—called a Walk-About—arrived, and I put it on her. Readers must remember that Shelbydog liked to wear things. So, after figuring out how it worked, we tried it. It wrapped around her body with a strap across her breast to keep it from slipping off her back and two handles that merged into one. While I held her up with my right hand, she went down the steps one at a time barely touching the steps. As we took one step at a time, I would say, "One." Once down the steps, I removed it so that she could move freely. I bought the sling primarily to help Shelbydog navigate the steps to the apartment we rented above a three-car garage outside Fairplay, Colorado. She was slowing down, often turning around, and heading home after peeing and pooping. She had a habit of lying in the grass and nibbling on it, when we met someone while walking and stopped to talk.

In late July 2024, after packing my Jeep with the things we would need for the month of August in the apartment in Colorado, we got an early morning start. Shelbydog was excited; she loved to travel, to go for a ride. On the way to our motel room in Pratt, Kansas, we stopped at a rest stop and ate lunch. The next morning, after gathering and loading all our things, we headed to LaJunta, Colorado, where I had booked a room in a motel. We got there early, and, after checking in, ate a late lunch and I took Shelbydog on a short walk. The next day, I reloaded the Jeep, put Shelbydog in the back seat, and drove to our final destination.

We arrived at the apartment on August 1, 2024. While I got the Jeep unloaded and put things away for the month, Shelbydog enjoyed the high mountain cool breezes blowing through the windows. In the evening I noticed that she was restless; suspecting that her joints were hurting, I gave her Tramadol, and she was able to fall asleep peacefully.

She enjoyed people who came to visit us, while we were living in the apartment. She also liked using the sling to get down the steps, but she didn't want to walk but a short distance to pee and poop. Then, she was ready to climb the steps back to the apartment. Both of us had to stop half-way up the steps and catch our breath. The altitude, which had not bothered us before, was affecting our breathing. She spent most of her time in a large overstuffed chair in front of a double window. She settled on a number of positions in that chair. Sometimes she curled in a ball and went to sleep. Other times, she propped her head on one of the chair's arms. She liked to lean on the back of the chair with her paws extended and her head lying on her paws, while gazing out the window. If she got too hot, she would slip out of the chair and lie on the hardwood floor to cool. In the mornings, she liked for me to open the door so she could lie in the sun on the stoop. Because it rains almost every afternoon in the mountains, Shelbydog was not afraid of the thunder that echoed loudly off the mountain peaks. All I had to do was tell her, "It will not hurt you."

While we were in the apartment, I reflected on the trust that Shelbydog had in me. She let me put the sling on her, then she let me help her down the steps. On her bath day, she let me pick her up and put her in the tub. Then, after wetting her and shampooing her and drying her, she let me pick her up and take her out of the tub. She trusted me to prepare and serve her meals three times a day, after putting on her harness, brace, and bandana every morning. She trusted me to take her outside three to four times a day so she could pee and poop. And at night she trusted me to put her to bed and cover her with a blanket, as I talked to her and prayed with her. She trusted me to understand her signs, like a raised paw or a sound she made. Her trust in me humbled me and inspired me to take even better care of her.

One of her favorite people, Matthew, came to visit for a couple of days. I had told Shelbydog that he was coming, and she was excited to see him. She spent a lot of time with him, even moving from her big chair to his bed to lie beside him before he got out of bed. After I got her down the steps, she went for a long walk with him; he was one of the few people with whom she would walk without me being present. She was sad after he left, so I spent lots of time with her, petting her head, scratching her ears, and rubbing her belly. Both of us enjoyed the cool mountain mornings—usually 35 to 45 degrees—and the cool, breezy afternoons—around 70 degrees. Near her overstuffed chair, I had placed a small electric fan that ran most afternoons to keep Shelbydog cool. One cool evening I turned off the fan. After a few minutes, Shelbydog raised her paw on the chair's arm, while facing the fan, to indicate that she wanted me to turn it on again—which I did.

One evening in late August, I went to the main house to have dinner with the owner of the apartment and some of her friends, leaving Shelbydog alone in our apartment in her chair with the fan on. When I returned about an hour later, she had taken the pillows off the futon and tossed them onto the floor. She had taken the pillow out of her bed and left it on the floor, And she had jumped onto my bed and pulled back the covers, but she was unable to get to the pillows. She was feeling well, and she was playful and happy and very alert.

In late August, other Colorado friends came to visit. After spending time with me and Shelbydog, we left Shelbydog in the apartment and went for a walk. When we returned, we had to gather the pillows from the floor and put them where they belonged. The month of August passed quickly. Some days Shelbydog was stubborn, which I understood to mean that she was hurting, so I gave her Tramadol, which enabled her to feel better and to sleep well.

We made our return trip from Colorado to Missouri in the same way that we had left Missouri and headed to Colorado: in three days after Labor Day 2024. After our first stop, I noticed that Shelbydog was in some pain, so I gave her a Tramadol, which helped her sleep well during the night. The next day she needed more Tramadol for the next leg of our journey. After we got home, she rallied again, wanting to walk a square block, something she had not done for a month. That evening I gave her another Tramadol. Throughout the month of September 2024, Shelbydog was on a rollercoaster when it came to walking. Some days she wanted to walk more, and on other days much less. Readjusting to the humidity was a part of that. However, she was sleeping through the night, which indicated that she was not in any pain and didn't need Tramadol. I continued to use the sling to help her down the front steps, but she was able to climb them back into the house. When I was giving her Tramadol, she was taking both long and short walks. When her friends visited and talked to her, petted her, and gave her bellyrubs, she was always happy. By late September 2024, she seemed to be back to her old self. While I didn't want her going down the back steps by herself, she often sneaked down them to the sunporch. Because she was wearing holes in her braces with her elbows, I took time to patch them in order to continue to use those expensive items. On walks I carried a bottle of water, so we could stop in the shade and she could get a drink. Whereas I had let her decide how far she wanted to walk on a given occasion, I began to turn her around after a square block and after a walk to the corner. I had concluded that going further and further was causing her distress, and I wanted not to cause her any more pain. I also noticed that she was tiring faster than she ever had. When we would get back from a walk, she spent a lot of time napping. By late September 2024, the weather had begun to cool, and that helped Shelbydog feel good enough to walk, to visit friends, to go for rides with me, to solicit bellyrubs, to roll on the rug, and to stop and roll in the green grass. The cooler temperatures gave her the opportunity to be outside more.

This continued into early October 2024. Shelbydog wanted to walk a lot. She was very perky, eating her food, begging food from me, being in the house with me, being alert, and being very responsive. I considered her behavior as an answer to my prayers for her deep healing. However, that responsiveness didn't last long, as her limp returned, and I began to give her Tramadol again. In my prayer, I asked St. Francis of Assisi, patron of pets, to interceded for her. To keep her from sneaking down the back steps, I ordered a pet gate to fit into the doorway. She didn't like it, and so she protested by going to the living room and taking things out of the trash can there and spreading them around the rug. By mid-October 2024, she had rallied again. We marked her twelve and a half birthday with walks. The cooler weather sparked the rascal in her. She was hunkering down, a sign she was happy, soliciting bellyrubs, wanting to play, and sneaking down the back steps when I failed to put the pet gate in place. In late October 2024, her limp was back. So, I scheduled an appointment with her veterinarian.

After a thorough exam by her veterinarian, she recommended that I begin to give Shelbydog Tramadol regularly twice a day, because she thought she was in pain. She also examined the stye on the edge and under Shelbydog's left eyelid. I had noticed it when we were in Colorado in August. At first, I thought it was something in her eye, but upon close examination saw that it was a small black thing attached to the edge and under her left eyelid. After examining the stye, her veterinarian told me that we would watch it, but nothing needed to be done immediately. If it began to grow and bother her, we would need to get it removed, as it could blind her. I cut back on some of the walking, just taking Shelbydog outside to pee or poop and getting her back in the house. With Tramadol two times a day, I noticed that she was feeling good, being more of a rascal, and wanting to walk farther than I thought was good for her. It was a real task to turn her around; I'd have to face the opposite direction, hold tight on the leash, and wait until she decided to turn around. I was trying to find a balance between walking, rest, and medicine.

By early November 2024, I noted that the Tramadol was making a great difference in how Shelbydog felt. While I tried to keep her calm, she was jumping and excited in the house, often even happily growling at me when she wanted something. After the switch from daylight savings time to standard time in early November, I readjusted our evening schedule to a late afternoon outing with a final pee break around 8 p.m. By mid-November 2024, her limp was back, but she was still finding a way to get down the back steps if I failed to put the pet gate in place when I went to the garage. One night she awakened me with a loud shriek or scream that lasted about fifteen seconds. After she got up and out of her bed, I called her back to her bed, talked to her, petted her, bellyrubbed her, and covered her with her blanket. I concluded that she had had a bad dream that had awakened and scared her. In a few minutes she was snoring. However, I didn't sleep well the rest of the night, because I was not sure what had happened. After speaking with a neighbor about this, I learned that it was common for some dogs, but that was the first time I had ever experienced it with Shelbydog. After that, she continued to awaken during the night, get up, stretch, and come back to her bed, where I leaned over and covered her with her blanket, and she went back to sleep.

In mid-November 2024, her restlessness during the night continued. Sometimes she would arise and move in our bedroom; other times she would walk through the house and find a rug to stretch herself on. A few mornings I found her on the rug in the bathroom, because it was cool in there. I began to shut our bedroom door, because I didn't think that it was a good idea for her to sleep in the bathroom. The first evening, she got up during the night and pawed the door; I called her back to bed. Closing the bedroom door became a regular part of my routine before going to bed.

In early December 2024, I thought I had achieved a good balance with Shelbydog with short walks, sleep, naps, and medicine. After it turned cold, she liked to join me in the outdoor sauna. She would sit on the bottom shelf, where I would give her a drink of water. When she got warm, she would look at me, and I'd let her get out and lie on the rug in the vestibule. Before I was ready to leave, she would reenter for a few minutes. I'm not sure that she liked the sauna's warmth; I think she just wanted to be with me. During the day, she was spending her mornings in the sun on the front porch. In the afternoons, she was sleeping on her pallet on the front porch.

She was also adjusting her circadian rhythm to correspond to the few hours of daylight and the more hours of darkness by going to bed earlier and sleeping later.

There were days in mid-December 2024, when she did not feel well, but with sunshine and Tramadol recuperated quickly. Even though our walks were much shorter, she stumbled frequently. Often, she demonstrated her rascal self, when I asked her if she wanted to go for a walk by hunkering down, her way of saying yes. She began to beg me to take her outside between 4 and 4:30 p.m. I concluded that she had received the deep healing for which I had prayed over and over. By late December 2024, Shelbydog had reached a balance between short walks, medicine, and food.

2

JANUARY TO JUNE 2025

IN EARLY JANUARY 2025, the balance between short walks, medicine, and food continued. Shelbydog liked the colder weather, and after it snowed, she liked walking through it in the backyard, when it was too cold and too slick to walk on the sidewalks. After the sun returned and began to melt the snow off the sidewalks, I was able to take her on short walks. When we would encounter a spot of snow on the sidewalk, she would walk around it in the grass.

In December 2024, while watching TV, I noticed an advertisement for Cherished Pets, a funeral home for dogs that had just opened near a local funeral home for people. Over the past years, I had been investigating local pet cemeteries. The one I liked seemed to be full, so with a friend I took a short trip north to see one, after having talked to the owner on the telephone. Because Cherished Pets seemed to be exactly for what I was looking, in mid-January 2025, I examined the web page and made a call to schedule an appointment. I discovered that the company specialized in pet cremation or burial on one's property, even though it was working with a pet cemetery a few miles away. After touring the facilities and speaking with a staff member, I discovered that the pet cemetery—Lakeland—that I thought was full still had openings. The staff member gave me the telephone number of the manager. I called him and made an appointment to see him. I explained that I was attempting to purchase a preneed plan for Shelbydog, as she was going to turn thirteen in April 2025. He told me that he would help me do that. I told him that I was interested in a green burial. He told me that Lakeland, because it was so close to a creek, was required to use a fiberglass vault. After all I had discovered, I concluded that that was as close to a green burial as I was going to get, if I wanted Shelbydog to be buried close to home. So, after picking out a plot and paying for the opening and the closing of the grave, I headed back to Cherished Pets to finalize arrangements. I explained that as Shelbydog aged, I hoped to wake up one morning and she didn't. I wanted to make only one telephone call to activate the preneed plan. I wanted to bury her with a red bandana given to her by a boy down the street who visited her often and gave her bellyrubs. I also wanted her cocooned in a pet burial shroud that I was going to buy for her. We got all the details worked out, and I returned home confident that I had put in place a plan to meet a need that I would use sooner or later.

By the end of January 2025, the stye under Shelbydog's left eyelid had begun to grow, and it was aggravating her. Her eye watered often, leaving gunk on her face. I called her veterinarian and explained that we needed to do the surgery. She explained that another veterinarian in the pet center did the surgery, and that she would prepare a surgery plan. So, we set the date to have the stye removed. My preparation for her surgery consisted in preparing a sheet of ten things her surgeon needed to know about Shelbydog Cole. I had said to the staff that I didn't want to drop her off and pick her up after the surgery, but that I wanted to stay with her before, during, and after her surgery. The staff had indicated that that was not normally done.

I asked to meet with her surgeon the morning of the surgery, and I did. I explained to her that Shelbydog had a thing in her upper left eyelid that need to be removed as carefully as possible. I first noticed it in August. We saw her regular veterinarian on October 24; she told me to watch it, as at that time it was not bothering her. In December and January I noticed that her left eye was watering a lot, stuff was forming in the corner of that eye that I removed, and she was rubbing it with her paw from time to time. That's when I decided that it needed to be removed. She had taken her morning medicines (Omeprazole, Apoquel, Carprofen, Tramadol). She had had no food since last evening. She was upset about not getting her breakfast after her morning walk (I hadn't followed the routine); she peed and pooped.

I had presented the following ten points on a sheet of paper to a staff member after we arrived. The veterinarian surgeon told me that she had seen the sheet and read it.

1. Shelbydog was a high-strung dog; she was easily stressed.

2. She had white coat syndrome.

3. She liked to wear things; she slept with a blanket.

4. She wore a harness, a double front shoulder brace, and a bandana all day. All were removed around 6:30 p.m. until the next morning.

5. She was not permitted to go down steps without the use of her sling, as all her weight would be on her shoulders, which give her a lot of trouble (including a limp). After putting on the sling, say "One" and she will take one step at a time while you hold her front end up and gradually lower her front paws to the step; then repeat the process until the bottom step saying "One" over and over again and lowering her one step at a time.

6. Going up steps was OK, because she used her back legs.

7. Do not let her run or jump; otherwise, tomorrow she will not be able to walk. Currently, we take three half-block or less walks on most days. She could not walk very far.

8. Please do not put her in a wire kennel; she will hurt herself attempting to get out. She hates kennels. Years ago she tore up two wire kennels and hurt and bloodied her mouth bending and breaking the bars.

9. After her surgery was finished, I asked that someone call me, and I would come and stay or sit with her until she regained consciousness. I would be the first familiar face she saw, and that would keep her calm, while I talked to her and petted her. If she awakened and did not see me, she would panic. I would stay out of the way.

10. She and I were like two peas in a pod. Wherever I was in or outside of the house, that is where she was. If I had to go somewhere where she could not go, she got very upset, because she loved to ride in the car. She trusted me (not to hurt her; for example, after she got a bath, she let me dry her some with a hair dryer; she let me take stuff out of the corner of her eye, etc.). She knew that I would not hurt her.

The veterinarian surgeon ushered Shelbydog and me into her office, and she told me that I would stay there until after the surgery. I had brought materials to read and work on. After going into her office, staff brought a small tarp, put Shelbydog on it, and the veterinarian surgeon gave her a sedative, while I sat and watched and talked to Shelbydog. Then, she gave her the anesthesia, and Shelbydog went to sleep. Then, the staff members picked her up and took her to the operating room.

I asked the surgeon veterinarian to take x-rays after Shelbydog was anesthetized, so we could see how bad her arthritis and joint deterioration was. She did. Later in the morning, a staff member came to me, showed me the x-rays, and explained what they revealed. Her arthritis was severe, and her joints were deteriorated more than I thought.

Later, the staff members brought Shelbydog back to the room in which I was waiting; she was on the tarp and regaining consciousness. I sat on the floor by her, talked to her, and petted her. When she tried to get up, I coaxed her to remain still and not put strain on her joints. After about an hour she had regained most consciousness, and, after putting a plastic cone around her head, staff helped me get her out of the office and into the Jeep. The staff made it clear that Shelbydog had to wear the cone for ten days to keep her from tearing out the stitches in her eyelid. After getting her home, out of the back of the Jeep, and feeding her, she went to her front porch and slept for a long time. We went to bed, and all hell broke loose. She couldn't find a comfortable place in her bed with the cone. She was up and down, keeping me awake. She begged me (whimpering) to take it off, but I couldn't risk her pawing her eyelid. Finally, she found a spot on a rug by my bed and fell asleep. After I got up the next morning, I prayed for help. My prayer was answered by Melissa and Jensen, who came to stay with Shelbydog, while I went to Cherished Pets to finalize her preneed plan. Melissa told me about an e-collar instead of the cone. After I left to keep my appointment, Melissa left Jensen with Shelbydog and went to a pet store and bought one for Shelbydog. After I got home from my appointment, Melissa appeared with the e-collar. She opened it, handed it to me to fill with air, and, after taking off the plastic cone, put it around Shelbydog's neck. She was so relieved that she lay down at Melissa's feet and fell asleep. The rest of that day, she enjoyed wearing the e-collar, because it supported her head, when she laid down.

My heart was broken the night before, as I watched her struggle to get the cone off her head. My heart was broken as I listened to her beg me to remove it. I was torn up inside and kept praying for help, and it came. While Shelbydog was the best gift that I ever received, Melissa and Jensen were the best gift on my seventy-fifth birthday.

The e-collar worked well. Shelbydog wore it proudly all the time. While watching her roll on the rug with it on, I noticed that it slipped off her head. I just needed to pay attention. The next morning, after she spent time rolling and wiggling on the rug, she appeared at my office door without it. She was letting me know that it slipped off again. So, I went to get it on the rug and put it back on her. If I had to be gone for any length of time, I had to have someone stay with her in case she lost it. Later, I discovered that Melissa did not read all the directions; a neck collar was supposed to have been threaded through the loops inside the collar before it was placed around her neck. The collar would have kept it from falling off when she rolled and wiggled on the rug. Nevertheless, a few days after surgery, Shelbydog began to open her left eyelid, as the swelling left.

Corbin dropped in to see her. And she solicited multiple ear scratches and bellyrubs from him. Then, she lay by his chair and slept for a long time. Her eyelid continue to heal, and, as it did so, it was easier to get out the puss and gunk that formed on it, and it was easier to put on the salve the veterinarian surgeon gave me for it.

As the last days of January 2025 passed, Shelbydog's eyelid healed, and we were able to take some short walks. Before that occurred, we went to the back yard, where she had designated a place to pee and another place to poop. She was feeling better, and she wanted to do more than walk in the back or front yard. She was happy when her friends stopped to see her.

Her surgeon veterinarian told me to leave the collar on for ten days, which I did. Then, I continued to put the salve on the eyelid; draining had stopped. I noticed some red in the white corner of her left eye, but it was curing little by little. She was feeling well and wanted to walk. When taking her outside, I often had to stop her from running.

By early February 2025, she had her left eyelid wide open and her veterinarian removed the stitches. That made her extremely happy. After that I had determined that she would undergo the Adequan treatment, consisting of two injections a week for four weeks and then a single injection once a month. Adequan was designed to stop her arthritis and joint deterioration. She responded positively to the drug with no side effects. Her surgeon veterinarian gave me eye drops to put in her left eye three times a day. After telling her that the drops would not hurt her, she kept her head still while I placed the drops in her eye.

Even through the mid-February 2025 snows, we walked. After a hefty snowfall of twelve inches, I had help clearing the snow from the driveway, while Shelbydog watched through the front door. In past years, she had been outside with me, staying out of the snow, and following me as I shoveled it off the driveway. However, this time I determined that the concrete upon which she would lie was too cold for her.

In early March 2025, Shelbydog's limp returned. I attributed it to the cold weather. In the past, after the limp manifested itself, we would take it easy for a few days and get plenty of rest. Usually, after a few days, she felt better. We were going to the backyard in the mornings for peeing and pooping, walking a square block after lunch in the sun, and taking a very short walk to the street corner and back before dinner. That daily routine seemed to work best for Shelbydog. I concluded that the Adequan was helping her feel better. In mid-March, we entertained guests, and Shelbydog enjoyed being around them. One of the guests was one of her favorite people: Matthew. She spent a lot of time around him soliciting attention.

On April 7, 2025, Shelbydog Cole celebrated her thirteenth birthday (about 82 human years). After five days of rain before with very cold weather, sunshine poured through the front door, and Shelbydog was happy to lie in it. Her friends brought her birthday gifts. With her dinner, I gave her a couple of pieces of her favorite milk bones. After she received copious ear scratches and bellyrubs, she played with her pillow on the rug for a while before settling into a nap.

By mid-April, she was not wanting to walk any further than it took her to find a place to pee and poop. By late April, the humidity had returned, and I attributed her reluctance to walk to the high humidity. Now, I understand that it was not the humidity; it was the pain she was feeling in her joints. We were having good days, when she felt better, and she wanted to walk more. And we were having bad days, when she did not feel good, and she wanted only to go outside, pee or poop, and return to the house. While I knew her age was causing her to slow down, I was not focused on her other issues, because she always rallied and indicated that she felt better. I'd forget the limp, and we would have a few good days of walks outside and antics inside the house. By the end of April 2025, we were walking only short distances.

I attributed her desire to walk only a short distance to the weather. Shelbydog hated rain; if she felt one raindrop fall from the sky or a tree on her head, she turned around immediately and headed for home. If the sidewalk was damp from a previous rain, she felt it and turned around to go back home. She didn't like humidity. Once it left and the sky turned blue, she was ready to walk. In fact, the dampness affected her arthritis and joints; a fresh, cool, humidity-free day made her eager to go outside and walk a square block. By mid-May 2025, after the rain and humidity cleared, I noticed that she was running up the steps after her evening pee-pee break to get back to her front porch. I thought that the Adequan was helping her. But once the rain and humidity came back, her limp got worse again, and I had to pick her up and carry her a short distance, sit her down for me to rest, and pick her up and carry her another distance. Sometimes, she felt like walking home, and at other times I had to carry her to the front steps. Her limp was getting worse. Her age was showing. She was sleeping more; she wasn't hearing the mail carrier put mail in the letter box or the delivery trucks stop at the driveway—at whom she used to bark. On the short walks she was stumbling, and there was not much more that I could do to help her.

When guests came to dinner in late May, I gave each of them a small piece of one of Shelbydog's milk bones to give to her at some time during our dinner. Besides begging me for a bite, Shelbydog went to each of two guests and got a bite from them. She was very happy, but spent most of the time lying flat on the floor.

By the end of May 2025, Shelbydog rallied again, and we were walking three times a day, sometimes two square blocks. I would attempt to restrain her, telling her that we needed to turn around, but she often pulled me forward, wanting to go farther. On rainy or humid days, we covered only short distances. On clear humidity-free days, we covered a greater distance, but no more than a square block. In late May she got what was her second to last bath, then she laid in the sun on her porch for hours. She was happy and excited, feeling good.

On June 7, 2025, I marked Shelbydog's eighty-third human birthday, according to the American Kennel Club's chart. She got an extra bone at dinner time. For a dog her age, this was a goal to be celebrated.

In early June 2025, I held a garage sale. In the past Shelbydog was always with me in the garage barking at visitors, greeting them—after I told them that she would not hurt them—and soliciting pets and bellyrubs from them. This year, I didn't bring her to the garage; I left her on her front porch, because I thought it would be too much for her to be on the concrete floor all day. She was visibly upset with me for not letting her come to the garage. While I was outside in the garage and she was inside alone, she went to the bookshelf in the kitchen where her food and bones were kept and took the bag of dental chews and carried them into the living room. She was not able to open them, because I had a clip on the bag. She also scattered many of her toys—kept in a shoe box—all around the house. While sitting in front of the front porch door, she barked at every customer who walked on the driveway. After the garage sale, I took her to her veterinarian's office to get her Adequan shot and to get her front toenails clipped. Because we did not walk much, her nails were getting long. Shelbydog was happy to go for a ride, even though it was to the veterinarian's office! On the way home, we stopped at the home of some of her friends, who came to the Jeep to see her.

Some of her favorite people came for dinner in mid-June, and Shelbydog got lots of attention. As I had done before, I gave each of them a small piece of one of her milk bones to give her while we ate dinner. She was able to roam around the table and get treats.

On Juneteenth, a federal holiday, her former owner, Corbin, stopped in to eat lunch and visit with Shelbydog, who spent her time at his feet soliciting behind-the-ear scratches and bellyrubs. He obliged her wishes, and both of them were happy to reconnect.

Because of the summer heat, by mid-June we had altered our daily schedule. Early in the morning, after Shelbydog got up, we usually walked a square block, unless she turned around and headed for home. Then, after lunch we would go outside so she could pee and poop, and we might take a short walk. Instead of going outside around 4:30 p.m., we began to go at 6:30 p.m., when the sun was behind the trees and we had shade. After the 6:30 p.m. outing, I removed her bandana, brace, and harness, and she would lie on her pallet on the front porch and fall asleep. She was rallying again. Before going for a walk she was hunkering down, excited to go, and she was playing with her pillow in the living room, lying on the carpet and pawing it underneath of her until it was pushed out, then she would use her nose to push it forward, and begin the process all over again, all the while breathing hard. I noted that when she felt good, I felt contented; God was healing her and renewing her life as my companion.

In late June, we took our final ride together, going to Joplin to see a friend of mine who was getting ready to mark a birthday. She was happy and excited for me to pick her up and put her in the back seat of the Jeep. I told her that this was the only road trip that we were going to take in 2025; I was going to take a two-lane highway to Joplin instead of the inter-state highway. Once we arrived in Joplin, Shelbydog enjoyed being in my friend's home. She liked to roll on the carpet back and forth. She enjoyed exploring his back yard. After we got home, we went for a two-block walk at her insistence, even though the thermometer was registering 90 degrees. I was surprised that she wanted to walk that far, but she kept wanting to go farther and farther. After getting home, we went to bed early that night, and Shelbydog slept soundly throughout the night, awakening me at 5:30 the next morning.

By the end of June 2025, Shelbydog was slowing. All walks were very short; after stopping to pee and poop, she turned around and headed for home. Her limp was back, and it was worse than it had ever been. She had to labor to climb the steps to get back to her front porch. One evening she came to the bottom of the steps and stopped. She looked at them, then she looked at me. "You can't climb them, can you?" I asked her. She stood still, while I picked her up and carried her in. When it was time to go to bed, I had to pick her up from her pallet and carry her to her bed. I began to use her sling not only to get her down the steps but to get her up the steps. However, after a few attempts using it, I concluded that it was easier to pick her up and carry her up the steps.

3

LATE JUNE–EARLY JULY 2025

AFTER I CARRIED SHELBYDOG to her bed on June 27, 2025, I went to bed, but I did not sleep well. I was worried about her and trying to piece together a plan of what I needed to do. The next morning after praying and reading, I decided to walk to Michelle's home. Not only did she know a lot about dogs, but she always stopped her vehicle when she saw Shelbydog and me walking and got out and came over to greet and pet Shelbydog. While we sat on her front steps, Michelle helped me sort the various pieces of the issue as to what to do. She helped me get me (my emotions) out of the way and make a decision that was best for Shelbydog. Finally, even though I was very emotionally upset, I could enact a plan.

I described what had been happening to Shelbydog over the past week. Michelle listened attentively. After both of us cried, she told me that I needed to call the Traveling Veterinarian; she had given me her number a few years previous, after I heard her speak about her and requested the number. After returning home, I called the Traveling Veterinarian and left a message after listening to her message giving her operating hours as Monday through Friday; she was not open on Saturday or Sunday. I explained my situation with Shelbydog and asked her to reply to me as soon as possible. I wrote an e-mail to Shelbydog's primary-care veterinarian, informing her of what had transpired in the past few weeks and what action I was taking. She and I had dialogued a few years ago about making a decision about Shelbydog's future that was based on quality of life.

I had promised Shelbydog, when she came to live with me, that I would take care of her. I accepted my responsibility for her, and, with Michelle's help, was getting myself out of the way to do what was best for Shelbydog, who was sleeping a lot due to the extra doses of pain killers I was giving her. I began to call some of her friends, and tell them that she was failing and if they wanted to see her, they should come soon. That Saturday afternoon some of them came to visit her. While she was responding to them positively and actively and was acting her usual self, she was on two different pain killers. I found myself making funeral plans for her; however, her excitement and peace generated by the pain killers she was taking questioned my judgment. I told myself that I needed veterinarian opinions. I was torn and didn't know what to do. When I talked to Michelle, both of us had a long period of crying; Michelle had been through this with her dogs many times before.

After sleeping well, because I gave Shelbydog an extra dose of pain killers before going to bed, the next day, Sunday, June 29, 2025, I reflected on being set free. That theme touched me deeply and supported me. While I was torn by what I knew I needed to do, I wasn't sure that I was prepared for it. I needed to grieve, to cry, and get even more prepared. Shelbydog had always been a free spirit, and now it was time to free her even more.

I made several phone calls to other Shelbydog friends, who stopped by to see her. I continued to reflect, knowing that I was going to miss her. In the *Shelbydog Chronicles*, I recorded that I would miss our early morning walks, our post-lunch walks, and our early evening walks to pee and poop. I would miss her scratching the bureau near her bed during the night to awaken me to lean over and pull her blanket over her. I'd miss her sleeping peacefully in her bed beside my bed, her snoring, and her wiggling during the night. I'd miss her visits from her front porch to my office during the day to check on me and to see where I was. I'd miss her afternoon solicitation for bellyrubs, while I sat in a living room chair to pray and to read. I'd miss going to her front porch to check on her and always getting her invitation to bellyrub her; she would lie on her side on her rug or pallet.

Shelbydog had been the center of my life for over five years—almost six. I would miss the daily routines of preparing her medicine, preparing her meals three times a day, and giving her a bite of food from my plate. I would miss piles of Shelbydog feathers (fur) in corners and walkways in my home during her shedding season. I would miss sneaking around corners to watch her play with her pillow on the living room rug, rolling the pillow from side to side, while breathing heavily in delight with her ears pointed up.

Often, I had acknowledged to myself and to Shelbydog that I had enjoyed having her with me for the past years, caring for her, and getting to know her. We had grown into faithful companions. I would miss her coming with me to my sauna in the wintertime; after walking to it, I would open the door and she would sit on the bottom shelf. After I got in and sat on the top shelf, I would give her drink of water from the bottle I carried, by pouring some into the bowl I kept for her in the sauna. Once she got warm, she would look up at me on the top shelf. I knew that she wanted to get out and cool off in the vestibule. So, I would hold onto her harness as she lowered herself to the floor and open the door for her to enter the vestibule, lie on the rug, and cool off. She had toys there, and she would often play with them. Before I was ready to leave, I would let her back in to sit below me, while I talked to her and petted her head.

While continuing to reflect, I acknowledged how difficult this process was to go through. Yet, I wouldn't want to give it to someone else. I promised Shelbydog that I would take care of her, and I had, and I would take care of her to the end with her burial and grave marker.

I knew I would miss Shelbydog on bath day, spreading the extra rugs on the bathroom floor, gathering her towels, calling her to come to the bathroom, taking off her bandana, brace, and harness and helping her into the shower, wetting her, shampooing her with Dog Wash, rinsing her, drying her, and wrestling her to dry her toes, then following her to the front porch, where I would roll her over so I could dry her legs and belly. When she first came to live with me, she hated getting a bath, but after five years she had come to enjoy it. I taught her that I would not hurt her. Then, she would dry in the sun. In the past two years, I had taught her that the hair dryer would not hurt her; so, she would let me dry her with the cool setting. Shelbydog was happy.

On the evening of June 29, 2025, a severe thunderstorm crossed over our home. I heard the wind blowing and went to the front porch to be with Shelbydog in case there was loud thunder; she was afraid only if the thunder was very loud. While 70 to 80 mile-per-hour winds blew, rain fell in sheets. Together we watched a river flow down the driveway. Earlier in the day I had attempted to contact the Traveling Veterinarian again, but got the same message as the day before and left an urgent plea to return my call the next day. After the wind and rain, the electricity went out; my generator kicked on to supply power to keep the air conditioning, freezer, and refrigerator operating. Internet also went out; and because my telephone was an internet phone, I had no telephone service.

Shelbydog slept well the night of June 29, 2025, because I gave her more pain killing medicine. I, however, tossed and turned all during the night making mental plans of what I needed to do the next morning. After getting out of bed, using my flip phone I called and left a message with the Traveling Veterinarian that the previous telephone number I had given her was not in service and that she needed to call me using the flip phone number I left her. It wasn't long before she called me; I explained what was going on and Shelbydog's state of decline. That June 30, 2025, morning I had to give her pain medication before I could get her down the front steps and into the yard to pee. The Traveling Veterinarian told me that she would come to my home at 10:30 a.m. I explained that I had a preneed plan with Cherished Pets Funeral Home, and I asked her what time I should tell them to arrive. She told me 11:30 a.m. Then, I called Michelle, who had expressed a desire to be present, and Corbin and Dani, who had also expressed a desire to be present. Another neighbor, who had visited Shelbydog two days before, came to the door and expressed a desire to be present.

At 10:30 a.m. The Traveling Veterinarian arrived. Before that, the five people gathered around Shelbydog talked to her, petted her, gave her bellyrubs, and kissed her. I told her, "We are going to set you free, Sweetie." My heart was breaking, as the Traveling Veterinarian and her assistant arrived and entered the front porch. The veterinarian examined Shelbydog briefly, looked at me and said, "It is time." I replied, "I know." After the assistant got the invoice ready, I got my wallet, and gave her my credit card to process the cost. Then, both of them went back to their van to prepare for the next part. The Traveling Veterinarian had told us that she would give Shelbydog a sedative, which would put her to sleep, and then prepare an IV for the final injection. After giving Shelbydog the sedative, Michelle got close to Shelbydog's head; she had requested to hold her head during the process. The first sedative didn't put Shelbydog completely to sleep. Shelbydog was tough, and she attempted to sit, but Michell kept her head on the pallet. The veterinarian gave her another dose of the sedative, and Shelbydog fell asleep. Then, she prepared the IV, gave her the injection, then took her stethoscope and listened for a Shelbydog heartbeat and shook her head.

Then, the Traveling Veterinarian made a paw print on a card, and a nose and paw print on another card, and gave both of them to me.

At that moment, I knew Shelbydog had died surrounded by people who loved her. As long as I live, I will never forget the feeling of emptiness that engulfed me. It was like a hole had developed in my stomach. I had already said my goodbye to Shelbydog, as had others in the room, but I hadn't considered it final. While we waited a few minutes for the van from Cherished Pets to arrive, we said few words, sitting mostly in silence. Two Cherished Pets employees arrived and entered with a gurney, picked up Shelbydog's body, placed it on the gurney, and covered her with a sheet. I handed them the bandana and cocoon in which she was to be buried, and they carried her body to the van. Before they put the gurney into the van, I asked them to stop. I went over to Shelbydog's head, uncovered it, and kissed her for the last time. They put her in the van, and took her to the Cherished Pets Funeral Home to prepare her for burial.

After all Shelbydog's friends left my front porch, I began to miss her. I missed her even though I knew that her spirit had been set free and her suffering was over. Even if I could have brought her back to life, I would not have, because she would be in pain or on drug pain killers.

That afternoon I called people who knew Shelbydog and told them that she had died that morning. That evening I went up and down my block, knocked on doors, and told all my neighbors that she had died. All offered their sympathy to me. I prepared an e-mail to send to people outside our town to notify them, but never used it. I began to call people one by one to inform them of her passing. I asked them to remember her with affection and kindness; she was my faithful companion and their friend for almost six years.

Somewhere in the midst of this process, I had decided to give all Shelbydog's things to the Humane Society. I had read an article about a pet owner who had written a last will and testament for her pet that included giving the pet's possessions to other pet owners who could use them. There were a few things that I wanted to keep in her memory, and there were a few things that I knew others had given to her that they wanted to take in her memory. For example, Corbin took two of her many bandanas. The little boy down the street took one of the toys he and his family had given to her one year on her birthday. A neighbor took the toy she had given her to remember her. I decided to keep her photos on the front porch to remember her along with her favorite duckie toy. Later, after speaking with a neighbor,

I decided to keep the coat I had made for her and use it as a covering on the bookshelf under her pictures. I also decided to keep the pillow with the pillow case I had made for her. She loved to play with that pillow!

After a call from the manager of Lakeland Pet Cemetery, I made an appointment to go there on Tuesday morning, July 1, 2025, to sign grave-opening papers. I met with him, signed the forms, and ordered a grave marker for Shelbydog with her name and dates of birth and death. Even though Shelbydog had been staying with me off and on before May 2020, that is when she came to stay with me permanently. She had been rescued from the Humane Society by Corbin in 2017. She came with a cloth bag of only a few items and two metal bowls. As will be shown below, she died with a Jeep load of belongings.

Shelbydog was the center of my life for six years. My every day revolved around her. Our morning walk depended on when she awakened and walked through my office. I always greeted her with, "Good morning, Madame Shelbydog," as she made her way to the front porch. Once there was enough daylight to see outside, I'd call her to come sit on her rug in the dining room, after stopping whatever I was doing, so I could put on her harness, brace, and bandana. If she didn't hurt when I lifted her right paw to slip the harness on, she would lick my hand. Then, we would go to the front porch, where she would stand still while I put her sling on. I'd hold her up as she, barely touching the concrete, descended the front steps, often looking both directions to see what might be going on. Once on the concrete below the steps, I would remove the sling, bring it back to the porch, pick up her leash and the key to the front door, lock the front door, descend the steps, and slip on her leash. Often, she would begin to walk down the driveway, and I would have to say, "Shelbydog, please wait for me; you cannot walk yourself." She would stop and wait while I attached her leach to the ring on her harness. Then, we would walk a square block or until she stopped, turned around, and headed home. But the last week, when she couldn't walk but a few steps into the grass to pee or poop, the front yard was the limit.

After getting her inside—she could climb the steps until a few days before she died—she would lie on her pallet to rest a short while. Meanwhile, I headed to the kitchen to fix her medicine and breakfast. After a few minutes of rest, she would come to the kitchen and lie on the floor in the dining room and watch me finish preparing her medicine and food. Because she would not take medicine, I had to place it inside a spoonful of canned or soft dogfood and give it to her in a small bowl. After she ate it, I would do the same with the next medicines. Then, I'd cut up the chews—because she wouldn't chew them and spit them out—into small pieces in her bowl with the rest of her food. Then, after putting a few bites of boiled chicken on the top, I would place her heavy, pottery bowl between her paws, and she would eat her breakfast while lying spread-eagle on the floor. Once there was no more food in the bowl, she would push it forward with her nose to let me know that she was ready for her large milk bone, followed by a piece of chicken jerky, followed by a small milk bone.

When breakfast was finished, Shelbydog would get up and walk to her front porch. She would stop at her water bowl and drink from the liquid with which I had filled it after I got up that morning. Then, she would go to her pallet in front of the glass door on the front porch and sit in front of me; I would be kneeling back enough for her to slip into her spot. Then, I would talk to her, scratch her ears, massage her shoulders, and kiss her, while we watched cars pass on the street in front of my home. After a while, I would get up and go to my office to attend to whatever I was working on. Once the sun rose, Shelbydog would lie in the sun on her pallet; if it were a cloudy day and there was no sun, I would turn on her light, designed to function like the sun. When she would get hot, she would get up, go to her bowl, and get a drink of water. Then, she would find a spot where there was no sun and lie on the cool tile. Once cooled, she would repeat the process.

Most days at some time during the morning, while I was working in my office, Shelbydog would arrive to see what I was doing and to get her ears scratched or her back scratched. Sometimes she came to my desk, and other times she peeked through the door, turned around, and went back to her front porch. Anytime between 10:30 and 11:30 a.m., I would expect her to come back to my office and request ear and back scratches; what she really wanted was her lunch. But because she was always too early, I'd tell her, "Go, sit on the rug, and I'll get lunch in a little while." She would go sit on the office rug, then lie, and then fall asleep. I'd hear her snoring. After she awoke, she'd go to the dining room rug and await her lunch, which I usually prepared around 11:30 a.m. She would eat it lying on the dining room floor, while I prepared my lunch. Then, she would sit on the rug by my chair in the dining room, waiting for the bite of milk bone dog biscuit that I would give her. When she was finished, she would either stretch out on the rug between the dining room and living room or go to her front porch. Once I was finished, I would go to the front porch, put her sling on, get her down the steps, and we would take usually a short walk for peeing and pooping purposes. When it was warm or hot, I usually carried a bottle of water; we would take a break in the shade of a tree along the sidewalk, and I would give her a drink out of my hand or out of the trough attached to the water bottle. Then, we would head home. I would go back to my office to work, and Shelbydog would nap on her pallet on the front porch.

In late afternoon, I stopped writing in my office and went to the living room to read. Shelbydog would find me around 4 p.m. either sitting and relaxing in a living room chair or sleeping in the chair. She would come into the living room from the front porch, lie on the rug, and roll over on her back with all four feet extended in the air. It was a sign for me to bellyrub her, and I would get out of my chair and onto the rug, where I would sit beside her, and do that for a while. Then, she would get up, shake herself, stretch, and go back to her front porch. If I was asleep in the chair, she would take one of her front paws and tap it on the footrest of my chair in order to awaken me! After reading for a while, I would get up and turn off the light in the living room. When she heard that switch click, she would get up and follow me to the kitchen and watch me, as I prepared her food and medicine. While she ate her diner, I would prepare my dinner. While I ate, she would sit or lie on a rug near my chair in the dining room and beg for a bite from my plate. If I was having something she could eat, I would give her a tiny morsel; if my dinner was something she could not have, she would get a tiny piece of a dog bone.

Our evening walk depended on how early it got dark. In the winter-time, we would go between 4 and 4:30 p.m. for a short walk. In the summer, we would wait until 6:30 p.m. We walked to the corner. In wintertime, I would get her down the front steps at 6:30 p.m. so she could pee one more time before bedtime later. In summertime, the short walk was her final time outside. When we got inside, I'd remove her bandana, brace, and harness; then, she could relax and sleep. Unless it was warm on her front porch, she would lie on her pallet, and I would cover her with her blanket. It was not long before I would hear snoring.

Around 9 p.m. I would turn on the porch light and awaken her, saying, "It is time for bed, Shelbydog. Come on, Sweetie." I would leave to prepare our bedroom. She would either come shortly or I would have to go back to the front porch and coach her to get up and come to bed. Once she made her way to our bedroom, she would get into her bed and form a bundle with her head supported on the side of her bed. I would come and kneel by her, take her left paw and stretch it out (she always bent it under her), and pray with her: "May God bless you and keep you. May he let his face shine upon you and be gracious to you. May he look upon you with kindness and give you his peace. And may the Virgin Mary and St. Francis of Assisi intercede for you for an abundance of grace that results in health and healing and lots of cooperation." While praying, I would place my right hand on her head and gently sweep it over her back. Then, I would lean over to her and kiss her head, while saying, "This is how much I love you." I would spread her blanket over her, and she would be asleep in just a few minutes. If I hadn't gone to the front porch to get her, I would go there, turn off the light, and lock the door. Then, I would go to bed. The first thing I did was lean over and touch Shelbydog on her hip, and say, "Good night, Sweetie. I hope you sleep well." Then, I would turn off the bedside lamp and go to sleep. The next morning we would begin the daily routine again.

Shelbydog died the day after a storm of seventy to eighty mile-per-hour winds with driving and pelting rain. The internet and telephone were out; electricity was out (however, I had a generator) for two days. We were able to sleep comfortably after the storm, because I gave Shelbydog a pain killer and we had a cool bedroom.

Shelbydog is woven into the fabric of my home. Wherever I looked, no matter what room, there was something of hers present. On the front porch, she had a rug, a pallet, and a water bowl. In the living room, she had a box of toys, which she often scattered around the house. In the dining room, she had a three-drawer chest of drawers with her bandanas, harnesses, braces, towels, and more. In the kitchen, there were her foods, medicines, and another water bowl. In the bedroom, her bed was next to my bed, and her blanket was on the chest of drawers near her bed. In my office, she had a rug upon which to lie. On the back sunporch, she had a rug upon which to lie.

The day after Shelbydog's death, memories flooded me. I remembered how Corbin had rescued her from the Human Society shelter in 2017, and, even though she began to live with me after, she still belong to him, until he and his wife moved to Florida in May 2020. I was taking care of her long before that when they married, as I took her to the wedding and kept her occupied with a leather bone. After the wedding, she came home with me.

While the memories kept coming, I took time to polish the Celebration of Life that was going to take place soon. I had prepared it in January 2025, after finishing the preneed plans for Shelbydog. Then, I kept my appointment to see the manager of Lakeland Pet Cemetery on Tuesday,

July 1. I signed the necessary papers to have Shelbydog's grave opened, and I ordered a marker for the grave. The manager gave me two options for burial, and I decided on the next day, Wednesday, January 2, in the middle of the afternoon. On the way home, I made a stop at Springfield Veterinary Center to see Shelbydog's primary care veterinarian. She offered me sympathy, and I gave her jars of chews and bottles of medicines that had belonged to Shelbydog. I asked her to give them to pet owners who could not afford them for their pets. I also thanked her veterinarian for all her help over the past six years. The only caveat I attached to the chews and medicines was that they be given to others in memory of Shelbydog Cole.

After getting home, I began to call Shelbydog's friends and tell them that she would be buried at 2 p.m. the next day. I told them to wear comfortable clothing in the heat, that we would gather under a nearby oak tree, and we would celebrate Shelbydog's life. As already mentioned, in January 2025, I had prepared a life-memorial service, and all it needed was a date on its cover. I finished the preparations. Around 6 p.m. electricity was restored, and the generator stopped running.

In the *Shelbydog Chronicles* I wrote: "Tomorrow I will bury a rascal Shelbydog. She was a rascal because of her expressions and her behavior. While playing with her pillow or other toys, she would breath heavily with her ears pointed up. She licked my hand when I took off her harness and brace to say thank you for being so gentle. In the morning, she would make a squeaky noise as she stretched before getting ready with harness, brace, and bandana for the day. When she was feeling well and ready to go for a walk, she would hunker down with her front paws stretched out, her head down, and her butt in the air. I often told her, "I like to see that butt in the air." During a walk, she would spot sprinklers spraying water over the sidewalk and on lawns and lead me off the sidewalk, into the street, past the sprays of water, and back onto the sidewalk. During the night, she would scratch the bureau near her bed to awaken me to cover her with the blanket she had wiggled from under.

After our morning walk and breakfast, we would go to the rug in front of the porch door. I would kneel and she would sit in front of me. We would watch cars on the street, while I would put my arms around her, scratching her ears, massaging her shoulders, and rubbing her belly. After a while, I would leave her in the sun or under her light and go to my office.

Memories continued to flood my consciousness. I remembered teaching Shelbydog how to push open a semi-closed door, like the one from the garage to the house and the one on our bedroom. I showed her how to use her nose to push it open. The word associated with the action was "Push." She got so good at pushing open doors that I didn't need to use the word. If we had been in the back yard, I would leave the back door ajar, and approaching it, Shelbydog would push it open to get inside the house. In the summertime, I would have the window air conditioner running when she came to bed. She would gently touch the almost closed door and it would open for her to enter the room and get into her bed with her tail held high to remind me that she knew how to open the door. When she opened doors, I often thought, "I need to teach her how to close doors, too!"

I had also taught her how to lie on the front concrete steps, while we often waited for our mail carrier, when the humidity wasn't too high. One day I helped her place herself on the top step out of the sun, showing her where to put her front and back paws, so she would not roll off. The next day we did it again. And the day after that, she had the routine down and ready. I often told people, "You can teach an old dog new tricks." Shelbydog was smart; she learned things quickly, and then practiced them often.

On the morning of Wednesday, July 2, 2025, I began to gather Shelbydog's things to take them to the Humane Society to be used where needed for people adopting pets. I began gathering her things from the front porch and taking them to a sorting table in the garage. I left the things I wanted to keep on the bookshelf on the front porch. Then I moved to the living room, then the dining room, then the kitchen, then the bedroom, and, finally, to the garage, where I had similar things sorted into piles. After putting similar things into boxes, I considered that I was ready to transport all to the Humane Society.

After finishing that project, I ate lunch and prepared to drive to Lakeland Pet Cemetery for Shelbydog's burial. I didn't know how many people would come. The grave was already excavated when I got there. I spoke with the manager of the cemetery for a brief moment and then went to stand under the oak tree. He had told me the day before that usually there was no one present when he and his staff buried a pet. I had told him that I would be there, and several other people had told me that they wanted to be there. Shelbydog's friends began to arrive and gather with me under the oak tree; there were twelve of us! I stood under the oak tree (to stay out of the hot sun) in amazement. The Cherished Pet's van arrived and the grave diggers helped escort Shelbydog's body—decorated with a red bandana and wrapped in a cocoon—in a fiberglass vault—covered with a cloth depicting dogs to the edge of the grave. After getting wide green straps under the vault, the three men lowered her into the grave and began to shovel the earth back into the grave.

The cocoon in which Shelbydog was wrapped was ordered from Sweet Goodbye; it was manufactured in Nepal and Bali adhering to Fair Trade practices, namely, to assist family businesses in developing countries, to assure the buyer that natural, biodegradable materials were used, and to support charities that focus on animal welfare. In the brochure that came with the cocoon, the manufacturer explained that the cocoon echoed both Native American and Aboriginal practices concerning the burial of pet dogs. The Pet Burial and Cremation Kit featured a guidebook that helped a pet owner farewell his or her beloved furry friend with a personal ceremony, because the pet was adored and missed, but never forgotten. The guidebook also contained complete pictorial directions about using the cocoon, words of comfort, and strategies for helping children cope with a pet's death.

While the grave diggers were burying Shelbydog, after distributing a program to each person in attendance, I led the Celebration of the Life of Shelbydog Cole. I began with a reflection on the biblical significance of standing under an oak tree. In old Bible translations, before modern scholars knew what the Hebrew word meant, what today is translated into English as oak tree was in the past called a terebinth. God appears to Abraham and others under an oak tree. A large oak tree connects the biblical three levels of the universe. Its roots reach down to Sheol, where the dead live; its trunk stands on the flat, plate-like surface of the earth, where people live; and its branches reach to the heavens, where God lives. Thus, all three levels of the ancient cosmos are connected through the oak tree. In other words, God biblically permeates everything he made.

After speaking about the biblical significance of standing under an oak tree and assigning various people parts to lead all present, while Shelbydog's body was being lowered into the earth, we began the following service:

A Celebration of the Life of Shelbydog Cole

April 7, 2002—July 2, 2025

Leader: Give thanks to the Lord for he is good.

All: His love is everlasting

Leader: We've gathered to celebrate and remember the life of Shelbydog Cole. For the first four years of her life, Shelbydog's life was hard. She spent year five in shelters. She is a survivor. In year six, Corbin adopted her from the animal shelter, and she was loved. In year seven, she began to spend most of her time with me, and in year eight she came to live permanently with me. That's when she was recognized as queen of the neighborhood. Since 2020, she has been my dog, although no one could own Shelbydog—she was and is a free spirit. She died on June 30, 2025, surrounded by people who loved her.

A reading from the book of Genesis (1:24–25, TM): "God spoke: 'Earth, generate life! Every sort and kind: cattle and reptiles and wild animals— all kinds.' And there it was: wild animals of every kind, Cattle of all kinds, every sort of reptile and bug. God saw that it was good."

Response: (Psalm 104: 24–25, 27–31, 33, TM)

Leader: O my spirit, bless God.

All: O my spirit, bless God.

Leader: What a wildly wonderful world, God!
You made it all, with Wisdom at your side,
Made earth overflow with your wonderful creations.

All: O my spirit, bless God.

Leader: Oh, look—the deep, wide sea,
Briming with fish past counting,
Sardines and sharks and salmon.

All: O my spirit, bless God.

Leader: All the creatures look expectantly to you
To give them their meals on time.
You come, and they gather around;
You open your hand and they eat from it.

All: O my spirit, bless God.

Leader: If you turned your back,
They'd die in a minute—
Take back your Spirit and they die,
Revert to original mud;
Send out your Spirit and they spring to life—
The whole countryside in bloom and blossom.

All: O my spirit, bless God.

Leader: The glory of GOD—let it last forever!
Let GOD enjoy his creation!
Oh, let me sing to GOD all my life long,
Sing hymns to my God as long as I live!

All: O my spirit, bless God.

Message: Biblically, God breathes Spirit into everyone and every creature he creates, dogs included. Nothing God creates ever goes out of existence, because everything and everyone—including animals—is enlivened by God's Spirit. Shelbydog revealed God to us.

Death is not the end; it is a passage to new life. Life is changed, not ended in the biblical world. Shelbydog's life continues in spiritual form. Her bodily suffering—acid reflux, sensitive skin, joints issues—are over. Death set her free from all that. Now, she is a totally free spirit; she has crossed over to spirit life with her Creator.

Yes, I—we—will miss her. I'll miss her awakening me at night to cover her with her blanket because she is cold. I'll miss her daily three feedings and two medicine preparations. I'll miss her finding me in the house, lying on her back with all four feet in the air, and begging for a bellyrub. I'll miss her walks, especially when she threw herself on the grass or in the leaves and rolled onto her back and wiggled and rolled and wiggled and rolled in delight and happiness. I'll miss her begging a bite of whatever I was eating for dinner after she ate her own dinner. I'll miss her running with glee through the house when I returned from an errand.

Shelbydog has been my companion—meaning one who shares bread—for the past six years. She was entrusted to my care by God, through Corbin, and she has taught me about unconditional love, about compassion, about forgiveness, about how to care for a dog, and much more. She was my teacher, friend, companion, rascal, muse, and the love of my life.

What she taught me will remain alive in me, and that means that she will remain alive in me. What she taught you will remain alive in you, and she will remain alive in your memories.

So, let's praise God for creating Shelbydog and giving her to us.

Leader: We thank you, God, for the life of Shelbydog.

All: We thank you, God, for the life of Shelbydog.

Leader: Lord God, we recognize your wisdom in all you have created, and we thank you for the life of Shelbydog.

All: We thank you, God, for the life of Shelbydog.

Leader: Lord God, we remember the unconditional love you have for us and all creatures and we thank you for the life of Shelbydog.

All: We thank you, God, for the life of Shelbydog.

Leader: Lord God, we know that nothing spirit-filled ever dies but is transformed more and more and we thank you for the life of Shelbydog.

All: We thank you, God, for the life of Shelbydog.

Leader: Lord God, while we are saddened at Shelby's passing, we trust that you have taken her to yourself, and we thank you for the life of Shelbydog.

All: We thank you, God, for the life of Shelbydog.

Leader: Lord God, as we bring her body to burial, make us more aware of our own mortality, and we thank you for the life of Shelbydog.

All: We thank you, God, for the life of Shelbydog.

Leader: Lord God, we praise you for your servant Shelbydog, and we thank you for the life of Shelbydog.

All: We thank you, God for the life of Shelbydog.

Leader: Ever-living God, we commit the body of Shelbydog to the earth, ashes to ashes, dust to dust. We thank you for all the blessings you bestowed on her in this life and on us through her. And we ask that you unite her spirit to your Holy Spirit so she can live with you in freedom forever and ever.

All: Amen.

Leader: Eternal rest grant to her, O Lord.

All: And let your perpetual light shine on her.

Leader: May she rest in peace.

All: Amen.

Leader: May her spirit and the spirits of all creatures through your great mercy rest in peace, Lord God.

All: Amen.

Then, with my right hand extended toward her grave, I invited everyone to listen to the prayer that I prayed with Shelbydog every morning, while I was getting her ready for the day, and every evening, while I was putting her to bed:

Blessing Prayer: May God bless you and keep you. May he let his face shine upon you and be gracious to you. May he look upon you with kindness and give you his peace. And may the Virgin Mary and St. Francis of Assisi intercede for you for an abundance of grace for healing, health, and cooperation, and today may God welcome you into his presence which you revealed to all of us. Amen.

Hymn: Now Thank We All Our God

1. Now thank we all our God
with heart and hands and voices,
who wondrous things has done,
in whom his world rejoices;
who from our mothers' arms

has blessed us on our way
with countless gifts of love,
and still is ours today.

2. O may this bounteous God
through all our life be near us,
with ever joyful hearts
and blessed peace to cheer us,
to keep us in his grace,
and guide us when perplexed,
and free us from all ills
of this world in the next.

3. All praise and thanks to God
the Father now be given,
the Son and Spirit blest,
who reign in highest heaven
the one eternal God,
whom heaven and earth adore;
for thus it was, is now,
and shall be evermore.

After we finished singing the hymn, I thanked all the people who were present. I thanked them for supporting Shelbydog and for comforting me. I asked them to drive home safely, and to keep the service sheet as a memento of Shelbydog. Finally, I invited those who brought flowers with them to walk to her grave and place the flowers on the earth that the workers had replaced after burying her. Then, all left Lakeland Pet Cemetery.

Once I got home, I began to record my thoughts in the *Shelbydog Chronicles*. Shelbydog was my teacher about unconditional love, compassion, forgiveness, dog care, and the ways of a dog. Shelbydog was my friend; she visited me often in my home office, sitting and lying at my feet, letting me sit behind her and wrap her in my arms behind the front door, while massaging her shoulders and scratching behind her ears. I loved hugging her and kissing her on the head, although she often wiggled free, because she did not like being enclosed by anyone or anything. She was my companion in prayer, often lying in my library-chapel. While I sat at my table to eat, she sat on a rug begging until she got a bite of food from my dinner plate. She was a rascal, being nosey and wanting to explore any neighbor's open garage, watching cars, and watching people do things. Shelbydog was my muse. She inspired me to write two books of *Shelbydog Chronicles*, and gave me lots of things to reflect about. Shelbydog was the love of my life. I had promised myself when she came to live with me that I would not fall in love with her, and damn if I didn't! She trapped me with her big brown, sparkling eyes, and her kisses, and I fell deeply in love with her.

Shelbydog was discerning. She would not let just anyone walk her. Of course, she would let me walk her and she let Mike, Neva, Kathy, and Sam walk her. But even when I was sick or recovering from some procedure, she would not go for a walk with a lot of people, unless I went along.

Her favorite walker was Matthew. When he would visit, she would gladly let him have her leach. Off they would go together. I would stay home and prepare food.

As already noted above, I read an online article about a dog's last will and testament. I began practicing that by giving all of Shelbydog's leftover medicines and chews to her regular veterinarian to be given away to people who could not afford them. I gave her leftover flea and tick and heartworm chews, along with calming powders, water bottle, and a toy to my neighbor for her dog. Corbin took her toy named Deerie and two bandanas to help him remember her. Her friend Jensen, took the toy he called Smiley, which he and his parents had given to her on one of her birthdays, and a water bowl pad that they had also given her. I kept her Duckie and the red and black bandana she wore the Sunday and Monday morning before she died. At the urging of my neighbor, I also kept the coat I had made her, using it as a cloth under her pictures.

I spent the morning before her burial, reverently gathering all her other things throughout the house. In the garage I sorted them. I went through her food supplies, removed things from the front porch, emptied her three-drawer chest, and emptied the shelf of treats and other things on the bookshelf in the kitchen. Shelbydog was everywhere in my house, and, while I was grateful for remembrances of her presence, I thought it was important to enact her last will and testament and give to the Humane Society what others could use and give the things in her memory. Corbin had rescued Shelbydog from the Humane Society, and I thought she would like it if I donated most of her belongings to it.

Besides other reflections, which will be presented in the next chapter, I considered the *Shelbydog Chronicles* to end with Shelbydog's burial. For six years I had kept a record-like diary about her and my interactions with her. I had nine volumes of fifty 8½" x 11" pages of hand-written *Chronicles* from August 27, 2019, to July 3, 2025. In 2019, I had promised Shelbydog that

I would take care of her, and with her burial I had completed and fulfilled my promise.

4

POST-CHRONICLES REFLECTIONS

THE DAY AFTER SHELBYDOG's burial, I loaded the Jeep and took a large load of recyclables to the recycling center, which was on the way to Lakeland Pet Cemetery, where Shelbydog had been buried the day before. After unloading the paper, glass, tin, plastic, and cardboard, I drove to Shelbydog's grave, prayed the blessing prayer I said with her every morning and evening, and just cried. How I missed her! Reasonableness thoughts took over my emotional response, and I thought about how happy her spirit must be in the next life to exist without pain and be absolutely free. After a short visit to her gravesite, I returned home and loaded the Jeep with everything I had collected of Shelbydog's the day before and was going to take to the Human Society once it opened after noon.

Around 1 p.m. I delivered a Jeep load of Shelbydog's leftover food, toys, sweaters, bandanas, harnesses, braces, leashes, beds, and more to the Human Society. I prepared a short note with my name, address, e-mail address, and phone number: "All of this dog food and all of these things are to be used by Humane Society Staff or given to those adopting animals who can use them. Please tell people that whatever they are receiving is in memory of Shelbydog Cole, who was adopted from the Human Society in 2017 by Corbin, who gave her to Mark Boyer in 2020 before leaving town. Shelbydog died June 30, 2025, at the age of 13+ (83 in human years)."

Humane Society staff helped me carry everything into the main building. They were happy to get such a large donation. After one of the staff produced an inventory of the items I had delivered and determined their value, I asked the staff to give away things in Shelbydog's memory. I emphasized that Corbin had adopted her from the Humane Society in 2017, and she would be pleased that her things were going to other dogs adopted from the shelter. After emptying the Jeep and receiving the necessary income tax form for my donation, I came home and began to record the reflections below.

The evening before, Michelle came by to visit with me. I had walked the sidewalk to her home, stopping to talk to other neighbors along the way. I knocked on Michelle's door, but no one answered, so I came home. I had just walked into the house and the telephone rang. It was Michelle returning a telephone call that I had made to her earlier. I told her that I had just been at her front door. She told me that she was walking to my house. After she entered, I gave her a copy of the *Shelbydog Chronicles* and *More Shelbydog Chronicles*—which she had discovered online—in thanksgiving for her talking with me the Saturday morning before Shelbydog's death, holding Shelbydog's head when she died, and coming to her burial. She told me that she was honored that I went to talk to her. She sat and we talked about dogs—hers and Shelbydog—for over an hour. Then, she left and returned to her home.

After she left, I recorded the following reflections. Shelbydog was known in my neighborhood as Shelby, Shelbydog, Madam Shelbydog, Miss Shelby, Sweetie, Beautiful, Precious, Rascal, Servant, Your Majesty, and Queen of the Neighborhood.

Shelbydog was nosey, especially loving to explore open garages, walking through yards, and smelling all around rooms. There wasn't a single storm-water drain in the neighborhood that Shelbydog had stopped before, stuck her nose in, and smelled many times. She desired a relationship with people she chose. She demonstrated her openness by lying on her side to solicit a bellyrub after smelling a person and licking (kissing, tasting) him or her. She would place herself at the person's feet or on his or her feet, until she got attention!

I was feeling empty and alone without her welcoming me home with a toy in her mouth and leading me to the front porch or the rug in the living room and soliciting a bellyrub.

Shelbydog liked Henry and Lauren, neighbors. She licked (kissed) Henry. I usually told him that he tasted good to her. She only kissed me when I was able to put on her harness and brace, gently lifting her front paws, without causing her any joint pain.

Shelbydog and I had a bond of absolute trust. We knew what each other was going to do. On July 4, 2025, I was missing her afternoon visitation to the rug in the living room. Once she heard me sit in my chair in that room, she would enter it from her front porch, throw herself on the rug, and roll on her back with all four feet in the air. Even though I knew she was soliciting a bellyrub, I would ask her, "What do you want?" She would roll a little more and stop when her feet were in the air. I would get out of my chair and sit next to her on the rug. Then, I would give her a bellyrub. She would smile at me, until she rolled on her side, and I continued to reach over her and stroke her belly.

If I left the room for a short time, she would take her pillow that stayed on the rug and scratch it underneath of her until it exploded out from under her. Then, she would nose it over and sometimes repeat the process. If she saw me watching her private play, she would stop and go back to the front porch.

After speaking to her friend Matthew on the telephone, he reminded me that I had initiated an intentional relationship with Shelbydog. As she was set free to be herself, she also set me free to be myself. That was the basis of our mutual trust. I had helped her overcome her fears of thunder, sticks (rods, handles), and baths by telling her, "Nothing is going to hurt you." She responded by trusting that nothing was going to hurt her. My relationship with Shelbydog parallels ideal human relationships: The pattern of love between two activate self-giving (sacrificing) adults. Such self-giving (sacrificing) reflects God. Through her body and spirit, Shelbydog mediated God to me, and through my body, I mediated God to her. The process of this relationship rippled throughout our neighborhood and beyond. Its effects are documented in the cards, e-mails, and flowers received up to three weeks after Shelbydog's death, and the desire of many people to return to her grave once her grave stone was installed.

I was sad and happy at the same time. I was sad that Shelbydog died. I was happy because she was no longer suffering, no longer on pain killers, and her spirit had been set free. It was a strange feeling.

After reading the past two years of *Shelbydog Chronicles* and beginning to doubt my previous decision, I became aware that her demise had been going on for at least two years previous. As her limp got worse, her veterinarian prescribed the latest in dog chews designed to keep joints working. Then, she prescribed one pain medication, Carprofen. Shelbydog responded positively. When the limp was bad, her veterinarian had given me Tramadol, another pain medication, to ease her pain. I lived into the future, forgetting the rough times and resuming our walking and playing. In other words, I realized that I was within the drama; I could not see what was happening, even though I was participating in it. I dismissed the hard spots and moved on. Shelbydog always rallied, and I did not become aware of her demise or deterioration until she was unable to climb the steps into the house. Modern dog medicine blinded me to her impending death, even though it kept her comfortable and out of pain. I was always celebrating her life and ignoring her impending death. As I began to realize this, I was comforted.

In the past, I had often remarked to Corbin that Shelbydog tried to communicate in all kinds of ways. Her friends often caught themselves referring to her as a person because she tried so hard to talk to them. She understood more when spoken to than many people gave her credit. I knew she understood, "Let's get you ready for your walk," because she would come to our staging rug and be ready for me to put on her harness, brace, and bandana, then on to the front porch to put on her sling.

After getting outside, while I returned to the porch to get her leash and the key to lock the door, she would begin to walk down the driveway to the sidewalk. I would say, "Shelbydog, please wait for me; you cannot walk yourself, Sweetie." She would stop. I would attach the lease to the ring on her harness. Then, I'd say, "Which way do you want to go?" She would begin to walk east or west on the sidewalk. Or she would head across the street, and walk east or west on the sidewalk. She knew all the routes. If she paused for a few moments after I asked the question, I knew she was waiting for me to decide. I'd say, "This way," and lead her in the direction I wanted to go.

I know she understood, "Go sit on the rug, and I will take off your stuff." Those are the words I would speak to her every evening after we returned from her final pee before bed. She would go to the staging rug, and I would remove her bandana, brace, and harness. Then, she would go to the front porch, lie on her pallet, and wait for me to arrive with her blanket to cover her. Shortly thereafter, snoring would be heard on the front porch!

As already noted, I taught her to push open semi-closed doors. "Push," I would say, and she would push the door with her nose. I taught her how to use her sling to get down the steps. As I would lift her slightly so that her paws touched each step, but her weight was not on her front shoulders, I would say, "One at a time," and she would begin to move to the next step. After saying, "One," over and over again, we made it down the steps. Before leaving the house to run an errand, I would find her and tell her where I was going and when I would return. I'd say, "You can't go," and she would lie on her pallet in front of the glass door on her porch. She understood what I was telling her. Shelbydog was very smart.

Shelbydog was also a rascal. I cannot remember the number of times I forgave her for her rascality. She would take items out of the trash can in the living room and leave them on the rug. She would carry a toy to greet people, as they entered our house. I had to instruct each person to take the toy from her mouth and then give it back. Once she got it back, she would carry it a short distance, drop it, and leave it on the floor. Sometimes she would grab a toy on her way to the front porch; after playing with it for a while, she would leave it there. Then, she would go get another, and do the same. I often picked up four or five toys on the front porch so that neither a guest nor I would trip over them and put them back into her toy box.

Shelbydog's rascality was also demonstrated by lying in doorways, often making it impossible to get through the door. She was a messy eater. Until I bought her a large white pottery bowl that could enclose her food, she left the rug upon which was located her water and food bowl full of small pieces of kibble or splashes of water. When she decided that she preferred to eat her food lying instead of standing, she would push the bowl forward on the tile floor to let me know that she was finished and ready for her large bone. She knew that at dinnertime she got a bushing chew bone after her bowl was clean and she had eaten two milk bones and a piece of chicken jerky. She would sit on her rug by my place at the table and wait for me to deliver it. Then, she would get up and go elsewhere to eat it.

Shelbydog was a theophany, a manifestation of God to people. She revealed God through her brindle coat with red highlights that glistened in the sunshine, through her big sparkling brown eyes, through her presentation of herself to others inviting them into her world through her presence. Even in her pain—hips, shoulders, arthritis—Shelbydog manifest the divine presence! She was safe, because she was a dog. Thus, she could kiss another or present her head for ear scratches or solicit bellyrubs by lying on her side. If another friend of mine, Jim Reynolds, were alive, he would have said, "How great God is to have created Shelbydog!" I often thought of

Wendy J. Francisco's song on You Tube titled "GOD and DOG." Shelbydog was a silent missionary, preaching divine presence without saying a word and converting many.

Shelbydog missionary work reminds me of Psalm 19: "The heavens are telling the glory of God, / and the firmament proclaims his handiwork. / Day to day pours forth speech, / and night to night declares knowledge. / There is no speech, nor are there words; / their voice is not heard; / yet their voice goes out through all the earth, / and their words to the end of the world" (Psalm 19:1–4, NRSV).

While talking to Corbin and Dani on the morning of July 4, they told me that they couldn't have found a better caregiver for Shelbydog than I. I asked them how they had chosen her at the Humane Society. They told me that they had gone there one day and looked at available dogs, but all of them were too aggressive. As they were leaving, they spotted Shelby in a corner kennel, practically hidden. She raised her paw, as she usually did. She was not aggressive. She did not bark. And she solicited a bellyrub from them. On their way home from the shelter, Corbin said they discussed choosing her. The next day, Corbin went back to the Humane Society and adopted her.

Shelbydog's raised paw—either left or right—was one of her most used communication tools. It was her way of saying, "Thank You." It was her way of saying, "I want more ear scratches," or "I want more bellyrubs," or "I want more petting," or "I want more food." It was her trademark. Usually, she would do it with a smile on her face.

I was grieving as I wrote those reflections. I realized that a part of me, the past six years of my life, had died, and I was struggling to bring new life to myself. My daily routine no longer was organized around Shelbydog. Love, companionship, presence, etc. was gone, and I needed to take responsibility to replace it.

On Thursday, July 3, 2025, the staff at Cherished Pets brought me the framed nose and paw print that I had ordered in January 2025, when I made the preneed arrangements for Shelbydog. They also brought me four extra nose and paw prints sheets with folders. I decided to give one to Jensen down the street because he was the only person Shelbydog let lay his head on her side. I decided to give one to Matthew, her favorite walker. After keeping one for an album I was making, I decided to give the last one to Corbin, her first owner who could not be at her burial due to a previous commitment. Corbin visited me on the Saturday after her burial to pick up the nose and paw print I had for him. I also returned to him the metal measuring cup for kibble that he had brought to me when Shelbydog came to live with me. We spent the afternoon and the evening talking about her. I would mention something I had documented in the *Shelbydog Chronicles*, and he would confirm that he had experienced it too. Shelbydog was the common bond in our relationship. I told him how much I missed her, but she was no longer suffering. She was now a free spirit. That didn't imply that I wasn't missing her presence and actions. It took me six years to get to that point, so I should not expect to go back to where I was six years ago before Shelbydog entered my life.

Shelbydog loved to travel. All I had to ask was, "Do you want to go for a ride?" and she was excited and ready to go. Besides going with me on errands, she also made four trips to Colorado with me; we visited friends there and hiked trails. If we crossed a creek or river, she was excited to wade into the water.

At home I had stopped relying on the doorbell or listening for knocks when someone was at my front door. I relied on Shelbydog's pattern of barks, which alerted me to the mail carrier, package delivery person, and anyone else at the front door.

To commemorate the first week of her burial, I made a trip to visit her grave. Before leaving, I went to my back yard and cut a pink gladiola blossom. There was no one at the pet cemetery. So, after placing the blossom on her grave, I talked to her, telling her how much I missed her and how much I had loved her. I said the prayer I always said in the morning, when I was getting her ready for the day, and in the evening, when I was getting her ready for bed. Then, I asked her to give me a sign that she was enjoying eternal life.

After I got home, I stood outside and watched a large black bird— possibly a crow—fly overhead high above the trees. I concluded that was Shelbydog's sign for me; she was freely living eternal life. I knew in my heart that was Shelbydog's sign. Silently, I thanked her for letting me know. Then, I went back into my home.

5

TRIBUTES AND GRIEF

BECAUSE ALL OF THE neighbors on my block knew Shelbydog along with others two or three blocks away in my neighborhood and even others who walked the sidewalks early in the morning, not to mention other friends in Missouri and Colorado, I had decided years ago that Shelbydog needed a dignified burial and that all her friends needed to know about her death and burial. People who knew her sent me cards and e-mails, which helped me grieve my loss. I also used *When It's Time to Say Goodbye* by Angela Garner (Rochester, VT: Findhorn Press, 2021); the author repeatedly reminded me that grief was the other side of caring, and I felt grief because I cared for Shelbydog. Garner, an animal bereavement specialist, presents not only material on grieving the loss of a pet, but she also presents valuable words on self-care after a pet's loss.

In the tributes that follow, you will witness the sympathy and compassion shown to me after Shelbydog died, and you will come to understand why I called Shelbydog the silent missionary in the previous chapter.

One friend sent me an e-mail, expressing his sorrow at hearing that Shelbydog had passed. He wrote, "I know that she had a great life with you. Also, I know you will miss her and her antics and her love. Be strong in the knowledge that she is no longer suffering." A few days later, a sympathy card arrived in the mail, stating, "Many thoughts and prayers are with you at this sad time." Below those words were these: "So sorry. Shelbydog will always be remembered and loved."

I had sent an e-mail to Shelbydog's primary veterinarian, whom I knew was not in the center on the day Shelbydog died. However, the next day, she wrote that she was sorry to hear that I had to make a quality-of-life decision for Shelbydog. "Based on the information you gave," she wrote, "it sounds like that was definitely the right thing to do for her." She added that "it was hard to see a pet not being able to do what he or she wanted and needed to do to participate in daily life, and when the joy of life is gone, it is the toughest and best decision to make. You did so very much for her and gave her the best quality of life that was possible with the chronic health issues she was dealing with. She was a sweet girl and will be truly missed."

In a card received from the staff of Shelbydog's veterinarian center almost two weeks after she died, her primary care veterinarian wrote, "Shelbydog was an amazing dog and will truly be missed. My thoughts and prayers are with you." The surgeon veterinarian, who had removed the stye from Shelbydog's eye in January 2025, wrote, "You gave Shelbydog the most amazing home—and did a good job with your first ever dog. She was so very loved, and she knew it. With heartfelt sympathy."

In an e-mail, another friend offered his "sincerest condolences on Shelbydog's passing." He added, "I know this is still so hard for you and for all the rest of us who knew her. I can't imagine how difficult it was to make the decision, but you provided such a peaceful environment for her to go, surrounded by her closest family member. Peace and love in death, as in life. She was so very lucky. She could not have wished for a better home." He asked me to call him to fill him in on the details, and I did.

A few days after the first e-mail, he wrote again, "I think you are right in that you recognized God revealing his presence to you through Shelbydog where most people would miss it. Shelbydog was a safe and constant way for God to manifest his presence in a way that you could experience every day. She was really quite a gift, and I would say that you received that gift with a lot of grace, and returned the favor by sharing her with everyone around you, as evidenced by the unusually large gathering at her funeral."

My niece sent me an e-mail, expressing her sorrow at the news of Shelbydog's death. "I know you loved her so much and she was such a big part of your life." In a similar vein, a friend who knew Shelbydog, wrote, "She was such a sweet dog and a wonderful companion for you. It's so heartbreaking when they die, even though we know this is normal and that she had a great life under your care. I pray that God will give you comfort, especially through the sweet memories of her time with you."

Cherished Pets Funeral Home and Crematory gave me a card at Shelbydog's burial that read: "May your heart be filled with memories of love. Forever in your heart will remain cherished memories. Our sincerest sympathy is with you."

Another friend sent a card expressing her sorrow upon hearing of Shelbydog's death. "She was so woven into so many parts of your life and in our lives as well," she wrote. "Her spirit is free, but we will carry her in our hearts forever."

A young couple a few houses down the street were welcomed to their new home by Shelbydog the year before, when they were moving in. Lauren wrote, "Shelbydog's light and spirit impacted us greatly, and we are so grateful for the time we spent with her. She will be greatly missed. She will always be the queen of the neighborhood in our hearts." Henry expressed his sorrow about the death of Shelbydog, "who in all ways (tangible and intangible) was a good dog." He regretted that he could not be present at the burial, but wrote, "I intend to visit her to say hello. I am grateful for the time that I could spend with Shelbydog and I hope she enjoys the flowers . . . brought from our garden (after all, she was very thorough in inspecting our progress in planting them). The physical world will be a bit dimmer without her presence."

The most profound words were printed on a card sent by another friend: "Dogs just know when they are loved . . . even at the end, when their pain becomes too much to bear and we help them to find rest," were the words printed on the outside of the card. Inside were the words: "No pet could have had a more loving home than the one you gave yours. I'm so sorry for your loss." The sender of the card expressed her thanks for my phone call telling her about Shelbydog's death. Then, she wrote, "Over the years I have had many, many canine companions, and while I remember them all fondly, a couple were very special. And I think Shelbydog was special for you. I have often thought that our dogs are the perfect example of unconditional love, a reminder of how we, too, should be." She added, "All who knew Shelbydog grieve with you."

The day after Shelbydog's burial I was surprised by a van in my driveway delivering a bouquet of flowers from Chewy, from which I ordered all her foods and medicines. "We're so sorry to hear of your loss," stated the card. "We know this time is tough. All of us here at Chewy are always here for you."

Two weeks after Shelbydog's death, other friends sent a bouquet of flowers to me, wishing me their love and sympathy.

Three weeks after he death, I received a card, stating, "The hardest part of loving a pet is saying good-bye. Hope it brings you comfort to know your friend's life was so much happier because you were in it." In a handwritten note, the sender wrote, "I am so sorry you had to say goodbye to Shelbydog. She was extra special, and the two of you had quite a journey together! She was and always will be family! It is so hard to let them go even when we know it's time."

All of those sentiments reminded me to bask in positive memories of Shelbydog, whose presence was everywhere in my home, but especially on the front porch, where I had pictures of her alone and with some of her many friends, along with other mementos. Before her death, I had asked a friend to take a photograph of Shelbydog and me, and she did; I framed that picture and put it with the rest of the photos. Also present with the photos were her toy Duckie and the bandana she wore the past two days before she died. All the pictures rest upon the coat I made for her years ago, when she came to live with me.

I do not think that anyone or any animal—any living thing—ever goes out of existence. Whatever God creates receives the breath of life, which, biblically, is a bit of divine Spirit. Throughout life on earth, spirit is connected to Spirit for spiritual life. Once the body dies due to old age and/or disease, the spirit is set free to be reunited totally to the Spirit from which it came forever. Thus, Shelbydog as spirit lives forever united to the Creator, who made her.

And while I bask in the joy of knowing that she lives forever, my grieving informs me that I need a new purpose. Before Shelbydog's death my purpose was to take care of her. Now that I have finished my care and kept my promise to her, I need a new purpose. I am lost, and I need to find me again. Do I need a new dog? I don't think so. I am too vulnerable and emotional right now. I need to live a year of grieving and see what God has in mind for me. Shelbydog was not a thing; she was not an entity alongside me. She was like a person with a strong personality, which cannot be replaced. She interacted with me, defining my purpose—to care for her—to which I heartily and gladly responded. My life and her life were so intertwined that they were one life with two dimensions: hers and mine.

By or in loving each other, we also loved ourselves; it was like looking into a mirror and me seeing her and she looking into a mirror and seeing me. That is how tightly our lives had intertwined. It was also why I was hurting and grieving so much; the other part of my life was gone.

Three weeks after Shelbydog's death and burial, I continued to experience an anxiety—a desire or feeling to do something—about something we used to do together. For example, after Shelbydog arose in the morning, I would stop whatever I was reading and get her ready—with harness, brace, and bandana—so she could go outside and pee and poop before coming home and taking her medicine and eating her breakfast. After eating lunch, I experienced an anxiety about needing to take Shelbydog outside for a short walk to pee and/or poop. And in the late afternoon and early evening, I experienced an anxiety about a final short walk for Shelbydog to pee and/or poop. I feel it again around 6:30 p.m., when I used to take her outside for the final pee before she went to bed. When I go to bed, I feel the anxiety again, as that was when Shelbydog went to bed and I prayed with her, she curled into a ball, I kissed her on the head, and I covered her with her blanket before going to bed. My anxiety was a feeling that there was something else I ought to be doing with Shelbydog. I have named my anxiety as missing Shelbydog.

Four weeks to the day after Shelbydog's death, I found a bouquet of zinnias on the steps of my front porch with a card from neighbors expressing their sorrow about the death of "sweet, sweet Shelby." They wrote, "She was a good and loyal companion. We know she was irreplaceable and you must have a big hole where she was." They added, "We surely will miss you walking by with her and Shelbydog deciding she would just lie down and refuse to budge."

Another card arrived in the mail. "There are loving [spirits] that leave their mark on this world" began the printed words on the card, "and once they're gone, those they've left behind are forever changed for the better." The sender, one of Shelbydog's favorite people, conveyed healing thoughts as I remembered Shelbydog, who was so dear to me and to the world.

The above tributes represent some of the e-mails, cards, and letters I received. As the days passed after Shelbydog's death, I came to a deeper awareness of how many people near and far she touched. That is why I subtitled this book *Touched by a Dog*.

As part of my grieving process, I found it helpful to identify (make a list) of what I missed (grieved) and what I did not miss. For example, I missed touching Shelbydog—feeling her fur, petting her head, kissing her on the top of her head, scratching her ears, massaging her shoulders, wrapping my arms around her, bellyrubbing her. I missed her smell and gazing into her big brown eyes. I missed taking off pieces of leaves and other debris that clung to her during a walk. I missed stopping at waste-water drains along the sidewalk so she could look into them, smell any smells, and on a hot day feel the cooler air rising from them. I missed crossing the side streets in the same places with Shelbydog in the lead. I missed her presence in the house, her peeking around doors to see what I was doing, being a canine doorbell—barking when someone came to the door, awakening me with her foot on the footrest of my chair after I fell asleep. I missed both the long and short walks with her. I missed her foot held up or touching me. I missed her lying by my chair wanting me to play a game with her.

Because I, like others, tend to remember only the good memories, I think it is important to mention what I don't miss concerning Shelbydog. I don't miss the daily schedule focused on her. Once she awakened, she was the focus of attention. I'd stop whatever I was doing, put on her harness, brace, and bandana, and take her outside for a walk; there was another walk after lunch, around 4 p.m., and one at 6:30 p.m. I don't miss the three daily feedings, nor the two daily medicine schedules; I had to wrap all medicines in canned, soft dogfood so she couldn't see or smell them, or Shelbydog wouldn't take them. I don't miss giving her a bath every three weeks nor doing a load of her laundry after the bath was finished. I don't miss being in charge of keeping her supply of food and medicine. I don't miss cutting into pieces the chews she needed to take for her joints and putting them with her kibble, because she would not chew chews. I don't miss the expenses of veterinarians, medicines, chews, kibble, harnesses, and braces. I don't miss repairing her pallet, bed, or rugs. I don't miss picking up masses of her fur during spring shedding. I don't miss being awakened during the night because Shelbydog had diarrhea and needed to go outside. I don't miss her stubborn streaks—when she wanted to walk farther (which she couldn't do) and didn't want to turn around, or when she would lie on a rug or on the grass and refuse to get up, or when she didn't want to come to bed when called. I don't miss her taking small pieces of trash out of the trash can and leaving them around the house.

I found it very helpful to sort my memories about what I remember liking about Shelbydog and missing her from what I did not like and didn't miss. The exercise helped me to remember all of the past six years in a healthy balance.

Also, I found it helpful during grieving to spend time separating emotional responses from reasonable response. Early in the grieving process, my emotions were stirred by death, absence, love, and more—all the result of having Shelbydog with me for six years. At times I was reminded of what a friend told me years ago about reaching good decisions. He said, "Ask yourself what a reasonable person would do?" And I found it a helpful balance to ask myself if my actions concerning Shelbydog were reasonable. While emotions gave me one response, reasonableness gave me another response. One is not preferrable over the other; one helps to balance the other in order to get a clearer picture during grieving.

This book is written for those who have read the other two books in this series. It ends the *Shelbydog Chronicles*. Hopefully, it also helps those grieving the death of a pet dog or any other pet with whom they shared a special connection. This book is for those who never thought of or treated their pet as just a pet, like a third party in a relationship. Single pet owners grieve deeply for the pet they loved and for whom they cared. A pet is a member of the family; and sometimes pet owners grieve more deeply for their pet than they do for human members of their family. Thus, anyone experiencing the absence of a pet, experiencing the emptiness upon the pet's departure from this life, will, hopefully, discover words of comfort in this book.

RECENT BOOKS BY MARK G. BOYER
PUBLISHED BY WIPF AND STOCK

Nature Spirituality: Praying with Wind, Water, Earth, Fire

A Spirituality of Ageing

Weekday Saints: Reflections on Their Scriptures

Human Wholeness: A Spirituality of Relationship

A Simple Systematic Mariology

Praying Your Way through Luke's Gospel and the Acts of the Apostles

An Abecedarian of Animal Spirit Guides: Spiritual Growth Through Reflections on Creatures

Overcome with Paschal Joy: Chanting Through Lent and Easter—Daily Reflections with Familiar Hymns

Taking Leave of Your Home: Moving in the Peace of Christ

An Abecedarian of Sacred Trees: Spiritual Growth through Reflections on Woody Plants

Divine Presence: Elements of Biblical Theophanies

Fruit of the Vine: A Biblical Spirituality of Wine

Names for Jesus: Reflections for Advent and Christmas

Talk to God and Listen to the Casual Reply: Experiencing the Spirituality of John Denver

Christ Our Passover Has Been Sacrificed: A Guide Through Paschal Mystery Spirituality—Mystical Theology in The Roman Missal

Rosary Primer: The Prayers, the Mysteries, and the New Testament

RECENT BOOKS BY MARK G. BOYER PUBLISHED BY WIPF AND STOCK

From Contemplation to Action: The Spiritual Process of Divine Discernment Using Elijah and Elisha as Models

Love Addict

All Things Mary: Honoring the Mother of God—An Anthology of Marian Reflections

Shhh! The Sound of Sheer Silence: A Biblical Spirituality that Transforms

What Is Born of the Spirit Is Spirit: A Biblical Spirituality of Spirit

Very Short Reflections—for Advent and Christmas, Lent and Easter, Ordinary Time, and Saints—Through the Liturgical Year

Living Parables: Today's Versions

My Life of Ministry, Writing, Teaching, and Traveling: The Autobiography of an Old Mines Missionary

300 Years of the French in Old Mines: A Narrative History of the Oldest Village in Missouri

Journey into God: Spiritual Reflections for Travelers

Monthly Entries for the Spiritual but Not Religious Through the Year: Texts, Reflections, Journal/Meditations, and Prayers for the Spiritual but Not Religious

The Shelbydog Chronicles by Shelby Cole as Recorded by Mark G. Boyer: A Novel

Four Catholic Pioneers in Missouri: Lamarque, Kenrick, Fox, and Hogan: Irish Missionaries and Their Supporter

Smothered with Inexhaustible Mercy: An Anthology of Poems

Spirituality for the Solitary: A Handbook for Those Who Live Alone

Seasons of Biblical Spirituality: Spring, Summer, Autumn, Winter

Biblical Names for God: An Abecedarian Anthology of Spiritual Reflections for Anytime

More Shelbydog Chronicles: Reflections on a Dog's Life by Her Friend, Knowing Your Pet

His Mercy Endures Forever: Biblical Reflections on Divine Mercy for Anytime

The Roman Catholic Lectionary and the Bible: Analysis, Conclusions, Suggested Alternatives

RECENT BOOKS BY MARK G. BOYER PUBLISHED BY WIPF AND STOCK

The Spirit of the Lord God: Biblical Names and Images for the Holy Spirit; An Abecedarian Anthology of Spiritual Reflections for Anytime

A Biblical Morning & Evening Prayer Manual: A Modern Book of Hours, Ways to Begin and End the Day

The Folks in the Woods: A Memoir of Brown Hollow, Missouri, 1874–1991

The Liturgical Environment: What the Documents Say About Roman Catholic Churches, Fourth Edition, Updated and Revised

Eavesdropping on Paul: Reading Others' Biblical Mail

Biblical Creation Stories: Plural Ways to Nourish Spirituality

Living with Grace: John Denver Spirituality in Song and Word: An Abecedarian of Themes

Spiritual Oxygen: Biblical Spirituality for the 21st Century